Praise for *What to Do About the Solomons*

"There's nothing more exciting as a bookseller (or a reader) than discovering a new writer who creates memorable characters in a setting we don't see every day. Funny, sexy, and smart."
— Judy Blume, *New York Times* "Summer Reading Recommendations, From 6 Novelists Who Own Bookstores"

"Like any Jewish story worth the salt that Lot's wife became, [*What to Do About the Solomons*] is admirably and quite beautifully rooted in 20th century history—and yet, at the same time, it largely steers clear of the politics that, from one angle or another, drag down so many contemporary novels . . . [Ball] works hard to render each [character] with sensitivity and respect, a dedication that also makes her fabulously unafraid to mark her characters with signs of psychosis and brutality . . . I ended *What to Do About the Solomons* absolutely swimming with affection, not just for the characters but for the multiple worlds that created them. Despite their collective penchant for psychodrama, there's something profoundly lovely—and loving—about the Solomons. And about Bethany Ball's debut."
— Alana Newhouse, *New York Times Book Review*

"A wry, dark multigenerational tale, full of emotional insight, about the Israeli and American branches of an extended family."
— *New York Times*, "10 Books We Recommend This Week"

"Big-hearted, fast-paced . . . Ball's debut novel is poignant and full of joy, as she weaves together the dramatic tales of these colorful Solomon clan . . . Ball has a keen eye for the absurdity of modern life, and a distinctive perspective."
— *National Book Review*, "5 Hot Books"

"A fast-paced, multigenerational, dysfunctional family drama that also bubbles over with humor and intrigue—essentially what you might expect (or hope for) from a tale of a kibbutz family and its scattered, colorful offspring. With beautiful language and sordid details, the narrative bounces from Israel to New York to Southern California and beyond (and back and forth), with plenty of gossip gone wrong and dark secrets in between."   —Victor Wishna, *Jewish Telegraphic Agency*

"As with any good literary soap opera, Bethany Ball's enjoyable debut is filled with fighting, betrayal, intergenerational misunderstandings, and a shocking secret or two."
        —Cathy Layne, *New York Journal of Books*

"Ball switches points of view for a mosaic of family members and associates in crisis and adrift. Her terse, sharp-edged prose captures settings ranging from an American jail where highest bail is king to a French military post where they haven't won a war since Napoleon, but they sure know how to live. For all its humor, penetrating disillusionment underlies Ball's memorable portrait of a family, once driven by pioneer spirit, now plagued by overextension and loss of direction, unsure what to do with its legacy, teetering between resentment, remorse, and resilience."   —*Publishers Weekly*

"Ball, with great humor, profound wit, and notable insight, vividly captures a singular family . . . This novel from a most promising writer has been compared to the work of Isaac B. Singer and Grace Paley, as well as Nathan Englander and Jennifer Egan. Try Eudora Welty with sex and Jews."   —*Booklist*

"In *What to Do About the Solomons*, Bethany Ball peels back the manicured surface of family and community to surgically expose a world of hurt. Told in a razor-sharp prose that takes no prisoners, this is that rare book that can make you laugh while it's breaking your heart. I couldn't get enough."

—David Hollander, author of *L.I.E.*

"Bethany Ball is a sharp, sensitive writer whose gift for details reveals, magically, whole worlds. She is both tender and relentless with her characters: her affection for them is palpable, yet she subjects them to exquisitely revealing examinations. In *What to Do About the Solomons* a family and its most harrowing moments come to life so completely we forget that we're not reading about ourselves and our own families."

—Nelly Reifler, author of *Elect H. Mouse State Judge*

"Bethany Ball lays bare the complexities of modern life in prose that has the resonant simplicity of a fairy tale. Readers who love I. B. Singer and Grace Paley now have another writer to adore."

—Brian Morton, author of *Starting Out in the Evening*

WHAT
TO DO
ABOUT
THE
SOLOMONS

WHAT TO DO ABOUT THE SOLOMONS

BETHANY BALL

Grove Press
New York

Published simultaneously in Canada
Printed in the United States of America

First Grove Atlantic hardcover edition: April 2017
First Grove Atlantic paperback edition: April 2018

ISBN 978-0-8021-2785-3
eISBN 978-0-8021-9072-7

Library of Congress Cataloging-in-Publication data is available for this title.

Grove Press
an imprint of Grove Atlantic
154 West 14th Street
New York, NY 10011

Distributed by Publishers Group West

groveatlantic.com

18 19 20 21   10 9 8 7 6 5 4 3 2 1

For EL and CL

SOLOMON FAMILY TREE

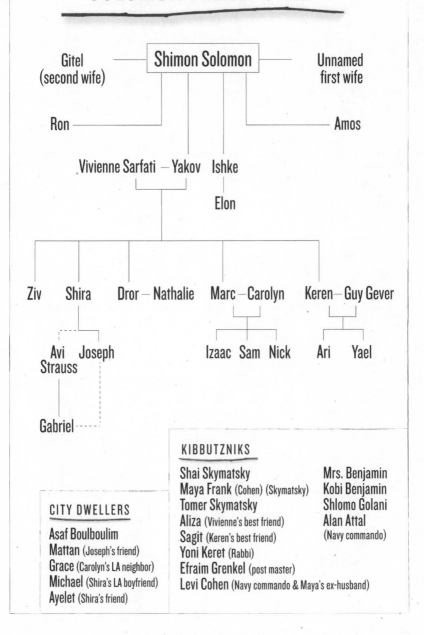

WHAT
TO DO
ABOUT
THE
SOLOMONS

Chapter 1

GUY GEVER STANDS
IN THE FIELD

N ow it is just a question of what to do with Guy Gever. For extra money he works in the evenings to frighten the birds that eat the crops in the fields around the kibbutz. At night, he hunts the porcupines, the dorban, and sometimes the tiny kipod, the hedgehogs, with his brothers. But now people think he has gone mad.

Before harvesting season begins, Guy Gever drives his pickup truck into the middle of the wheat. In the center of the field, he arranges the sticks and branches he pulls from the back of the pickup. He arranges and rearranges them until the sun comes up. He spreads birdseed all around. The birds come from the Kinneret to the north and the Dead Sea to the south. They fly over Americans and Africans in white robes baptizing themselves in the Jordan. They come from Syria and Lebanon, but not the West Bank or Gaza, where there are no birds.

Guy Gever stands in the middle of the field and counts and names each bird as they come. A helicopter flies overhead and bathes them in a shower of pesticide. Someone calls the police. He can see them coming over the highway. He hops into his truck and drives off. For a few days no one knows where he's gone.

Later that week, a group of kibbutzniks sees him stacking cypress branches off the side of the highway, on their way to Hamat Gader, the hot springs. Come on, Guy! Come with us, they shout. Leave the bush in the ground and the sticks on the trees and take a rest.

I have had enough leisure, Guy Gever says. He climbs into the back of the pickup truck and salutes them. Now I must work.

Guy Gever's father-in-law, Yakov Solomon, runs his hands through his still black hair and nods. He strokes his sideburns. The parliament of old men, the sabras, sit around a barbecue pit with a bottle of whiskey and discuss Guy Gever. They pass the bottle and pour drabs into dusty tea glasses. Yakov sets his glass on the ground, wedging it into the dirt. He crosses his arms high across his narrow chest. Yes, Yakov says. This is true. Guy Gever has had enough leisure time. I should know. I bought his cars, financed renovations on houses I paid for, and covered all medical costs for Guy Gever's son. When my children want money, they come to me. When their children need money, they come to me. The men nod. They defer to him, to Yakov Solomon, the most powerful man in the Jordan River Valley. I paid for their bar mitzvahs, their educations, and their therapists. I've paid for six weddings, five divorces, the funeral of one daughter-in-law's father, and countless birthday celebrations. Now I must pay for Guy Gever's madness?

The men nod and grunt and drink to Yakov Solomon.

Guy Gever hears about the parliament from his younger brother, Itai, who heard it from Elon, who is the son of Yakov's middle brother Ishke. Guy Gever squats down to the ground and spits. He draws a woman in the dirt with his finger. He stands up and shouts, That man! For ten years I've been Yakov Solomon's slave. Why doesn't he die already?

And leave everything to you, says Itai, who is lo gamur, not finished, funny in the head. That would be something.

Yakov Solomon and his wife, Vivienne, drive from the kibbutz to Jerusalem to meet their children. Vivienne tells her husband, We must keep this very quiet, for Keren's sake, and for the children. We mustn't tell anyone. Guy will never find a job again. Who does he think he is? An artist? *Phoot!* He has gone mad! We must hire a private doctor. Send him to America, perhaps. Aliza tells me in America they have more mental hospitals than regular ones!

Yakov listens to his wife with increasing irritation. He presses his foot hard on the accelerator. He goes too fast, but he is nearly seventy-five years old, and anyway, he is going to die eventually. Better to do so in a blaze of concrete, steel, and light. I'm done with Guy Gever and all the rest of them! I should have cut them off years ago. The jobs! The connections! The money! Offer them a finger and they want the whole hand!

Yakov, Vivienne says. You were the one who said, "Keep the seeds in your pocket and give it to the birds one by one."

Yes! Keep the birds close so they don't fly away. Spit flies from his mouth. But now, they can go fuck themselves!

Maya, on an airplane flying back from Amsterdam, is unaware of Guy Gever and his troubles. If someone mentioned his name to her, she would hardly be able to summon a face. If she thought hard enough, she might remember a tall, slight boy with light, straight hair parted across his forehead, strategically arranged to draw attention away from his long, thin nose. Then again, she might get him confused with someone else. Soft, slow Kobi Benjamin, for instance. She may or may not remember that Guy Gever married the sister of her first love: Marc Solomon.

Even if she knew, Maya no longer cares about who has gone crazy on the kibbutz. But she doesn't know. Her mother stopped telling her anything years ago.

I am on my way home, Maya thinks, and she feels dread in her chest.

At dinner in a newly opened Jerusalem restaurant with his son Dror and daughter Shira, Yakov Solomon rails against Guy Gever: I always knew he was trouble! What will I do now? What can be done? I can't even grow old and die in peace!

Dror asks, What do you mean what will you do? It's not for you to do anything! Let them sort it out on their own.

It will all fall on me! I will have to support Keren and the children and God knows who else!

Dror says, Why? They are grown-ups! Guy Gever is a grown man!

Ach! cries Yakov. He yanks on a bit of hair. You don't know what I've done for that man.

What are you saying? Dror shouts. I know what you've done for him!

Dror's sister Shira puts her head in her hands.

Dror says, I come to the kibbutz once every month and you only ever sit with Guy Gever. You completely ignored us all these years. You elevated Guy to a god. You could never see his faults. We saw them. Only you and Keren were blind to Guy Gever. He's been *crazy* for years!

Yakov grows cold. He sits with his arms crossed high over his chest and pulls on his moustache. Children play in the courtyard around the restaurant. A dog barks and another distant dog answers. Dror's wife leans toward Dror and murmurs words no one at the table can hear. I cannot imagine, Yakov says, at your age, to be so jealous. Such a childish emotion is jealousy.

They sit in silence.

Dror smiles at his father. You are an irascible old son of a bitch.

But Yakov is no longer listening. He nods and stares out at the street lamps. One blinks on and off. Yakov strokes the whiskers on his chin. The coarse hairs soothe his fingers. Yes, it's true, he thinks. Of all my three sons, it was Guy I loved the best. The one who was not my son. The only one I could talk to. Now, it has all gone to shit.

The next day, Yakov and Vivienne share a late breakfast with Shira. She is the fourth child. The baby until Marc came along. At Café Mitzrachi near the shuk, Yakov and Shira eat their omelets and salad and hatch a plan.

Watching Shira, Vivienne chortles to herself. They are made for each other, Shira and Yakov. He's sired the perfect mate for himself. Vivienne sits silently. If she spoke, it wouldn't make any difference. As the Solomon matriarch, almost no one talks to her anymore. Only Guy Gever ever thanked her for the Friday meals she makes. What a joke it is: The two least stable in her family, Yakov and Shira, deciding the fate of a man who has lost all reason. If only Ziv were here, the oldest. Or Marc, the youngest.

Of all her children, Ziv is the most rational, and the kindest.

Let us not talk of Ziv, Vivienne thinks to herself. Living with another *man* in Singapore.

Vivienne prays daily. She once prayed for sanity and peace but now she prays that Guy Gever will give up his ridiculous artistic pretensions and go back to work. Vivienne prays that everyone will grow to be as wise as she is. She touches her hair and thinks of having it hennaed.

Guy Gever drives his truck all the way to Sfat in the north to see a specialist. Keren sits beside him. The hospital is modern cement and crumbling. It is my family that is crazy, Professor, he says, very quietly, very controlled, to the inscrutable doctor with the stone face. The doctor nods and scribbles his notes.

When they return to the kibbutz, Keren tells her mother what the doctor had said: *He is enjoying himself. He enjoys doing whatever he likes.*

6

Later, on the telephone, Vivienne tells Shira, Guy Gever has always enjoyed doing whatever he likes! Who has been raising the children? Who cooked every Friday dinner? Who did Keren come crying to when Guy was out gallivanting with that Russian's wife? Who supported him through school?

Yes, Dror says, three days later, sitting in a restaurant outside Tiberias with his parents and Shira. And who paid all the bills!

And yours too, Vivienne says.

Dror opens his mouth and then shuts it again. Vivienne and Yakov say nothing. Everyone sits very still on the patio outside the restaurant. The Kinneret is quiet. Seagulls fight over a container of fries someone has left on the small stones of the beach. The lights of Tiberias glow in the distance behind them. The Kinneret—the biblical Sea of Galilee—is gentle on the shore. In years of drought, the sea recedes and leaves a vast beach. This is a year of drought.

Vivienne squares her shoulders and sits up tall. Her hair is a beacon of the brightest red. None of you children have ever really supported yourselves. We are always here. We are your safety net.

Except for Marc, she thinks. Her favorite son. In New York. And Ziv.

Vivienne thinks of Ziv, and winces. Ziv was the most beautiful and intelligent of the children. The firstborn son. The perfect combination of Yakov and Vivienne and then—

What is it, Ima? Shira asks.

Rien, Vivienne says. Nothing of any matter.

✵   ✵   ✵

BETHANY BALL

The fields are shorn. They burn in the terrible late spring sun. Guy Gever has spent a week laying pulled-up shrubs along the median in the center of the road that leads to Beit She'an.

Yakov calls Marc in America. He says, Come back to the kibbutz. Go sit with Guy. Talk to him.

Abba, says Marc, Guy never liked me. We don't know each other that well. By the time Keren married him, I was already in the army. Have Ziv come from Singapore. He is the oldest. He was always the peacekeeper. Marc says, I am busy with the move to Los Angeles.

Never mind! Yakov says.

Marc hangs up the phone. Guy is of another type altogether, Marc thinks sitting in his New York office. Guy and his brothers, running around the fields all summer long shooting wild porcupine—a Gever speciality—skinning them and then roasting them on spits. During Shavuot, the harvesting festival, when the children would go at night into the wheat fields alone, Guy Gever and his friends would impale the heads of slaughtered cows on stakes. Marc stumbled over one when he was ten and the image of it with its filmed-over eyes, and terrible mouth hanging open, still greets him in the night. Those menacing fields of the Shavuot holidays! Those Gevers! They are the joke of the kibbutzniks. In the army, Marc was a commando and Guy Gever, a what? A thug in Gaza!

Guy Gever drives up to his house in his pickup. He has just returned from the Valley where he has been digging up the small ancient trees.

No, doctor, Guy says to himself, the bushes don't *talk* to me. I don't hear *voices*. I am not Moses! I am not Yeshua! There is no burning bush! The soil and roots and trees guide me where to place them. They vibrate in a particular way. The art of placement is divine. Like the Kotel is divine. Like Stonehenge. Like Petra.

He stacks the branches around the house he shares with Keren. He piles the cypress as high as the windows.

Keren lies in bed with a migraine. She hears the rumble of the truck, and the joy she felt for the last twelve years of marriage is replaced with dread. The sleeping medicine she took gives her strange dreams. Bondormin, it's called. She imagines that Guy has walled her in. She hears sounds outside. She sits up in bed and reaches over to push aside the curtain but sees only her reflection in the dark glass. Her eyes refocus and she sees cut cypress branches pressed against the other side of the window. Keren gasps and claws at the glass. Keren, she hears. She turns from the window to the door of her bedroom and Guy's face, his strange feral face, hovers over her. Keren screams.

Guy gently takes hold of Keren's hands and pulls her up to sitting. Oh, Keren, he says. Don't you love me anymore? She melts a little, and relents to his hands. He hasn't spoken to her so gently since her thirtieth birthday, when they'd gone to the tzimmer with the hot tubs and king-size beds and decided that they would try for another baby. Their youngest child is already seven years old. Wouldn't she like another? He holds her hands and leads her past their living room to the outside

9

patio. She starts to speak but he puts two fingers over her lips and kisses her.

The moon is so high it looks electric. It illuminates the cypress trees that stand guard in the kibbutz and in the fields beyond.

Keren in her nightgown. It billows around her ankles. The hammock swings on the porch. They stand together on the front patio. It is a perfect, dry Jordan Valley night.

Keren's sister, Shira, takes a bus back to Jerusalem. Avi Strauss, the handsome, fat producer of the comedy news program *Hamesh*, waits for her outside the bus station. He leans back against his black chauffeured SUV. He's left his cane inside the car. He wants to appear virile. Shira is touched.

They drive into the heart of Jerusalem into the Old City and the restaurants in the Christian Quarter. The driver parks beside an old establishment restaurant. Inside, there are sheikhs and wizened ex–prime ministers. Shira has gone there many times with her father. The last time she was there with Avi, they saw Ariel Sharon there, that old walrus, and Avi had hissed at him. Sharon had laughed and sent over cognac.

Now, seated at the table, Avi Strauss looks at her, cups her face in his hands. He is almost seventy years old. Shira is twenty-five. Shira is in love. She feels like a very young girl, like a teenager before the army. Young women, Avi says, get the best of old men. We are our most charming trying to impress them.

In his apartment in the Russian Compound neighborhood he is very full, and farting. He looks at her apologetically. She would like to have a child. She will try and get pregnant. He would marry her if not for his wife and their four children.

Alas, he cannot perform. Tonight is not the night she will conceive. Flooded with sympathy, she pats his hand as they lie beside one another in his bed. Tomorrow night. Tomorrow night I will make up for it, he says. She knows he will. His large bloated belly is like a third person in the bed. He goes down on her. He tells her, I won't inflict Viagra on you.

Two years earlier, at a film premiere at the Ambassadors' Club, he had seduced her by saying he would make a television show for her to star in. He knows people in America. She fell for him, though she knows now the show will never be made. A year from now, he will finish a movie that will win at Cannes. Shira will have a small role for which she will be paid handsomely—more even than the lead actress. He will break up with her, take his wife and nearly grown children across the world, and die in the bed of an underage stripper somewhere in the San Fernando Valley.

Guy Gever and Keren make love in the hammock. They hunker down low into one another, putting all their weight into the fabric at the center of the hammock so it doesn't pitch them out. The frequently beaten eight-year-old who lives next door and is up all hours of the night watches from his window. Guy wonders if the eight-year-old is his son. Did he ever fuck his mother? No, but he wanted to. Guy would like to adopt the child and take him to Petra, in Jordan, where the red rocks are. He had been to Jordan once, on a secret military mission for which he'd been the driver. A relief after all those months in the territories, and the red cliffs have haunted him ever since.

Dawn comes and Guy and Keren wake up entwined and stiff in the hammock. Morning dew and sweat have made them damp. Guy agrees to go again to a doctor. He shakes his head. But I'm not crazy, he says. I am an artist. Must everything be work and war and commerce?

This time the doctor's office is located in a Druze village. This way, no one in the kibbutz will know. The neighbors will not know. The doctor is supposed to be very good. He is revered by the Christian and Druze communities.

Guy Gever and Keren drive together through the hills and up the lonely canyon roads. The building is low and modern on the outskirts of the village. The doctor reads from a standard questionnaire: Do you think you are the Messiah? Do you hear voices?

What number question is that? Guy asks the doctor. The doctor has blue eyes and is named Josef.

Sixteen, the doctor says.

Guy Gever watches the doctor's finger slide across the paper as he makes his little notes. Sixteen is a crucial number, Guy thinks. In every pile from this point onward, there will be sixteen branches of eucalyptus tree.

*　*　*

Maya has come back to the kibbutz from Amsterdam after finding neither fame nor fortune. What a relief it had been to live among the peaceful Europeans. So much better than the unrepentant kibbutzniks who watch the rockets fall into Beit She'an but take no responsibility. In Amsterdam, there was hash and there was pain and then a solid march to opiates, and on the cycle went. She was beautiful and talented still. Everyone in the kibbutz had thought she would one day be famous. She might even have gone to America where her father has lived since she was a child. Her father whom she has not heard from in ten years or more. But America was the only place anyone went and made anything of themselves. Even the Russians she teaches in her government ulpan job confide in her that they are only in Israel as a way to get to America. She might have gone too if not for the ease of her Dutch passport. The passport as token prize of Holocaust survivor relatives notwithstanding: The Dutch did hate their foreigners. Her dreadlocked hair dyed platinum blond, with dark black roots, her black eyes and tiny, straight figure. Slim and boyish. Passport or no, she would never really be Dutch.

At midnight, she leaves her mother's house with her iPod. She plugs the earbuds deep into her ears and blasts the music she used to listen to back in Amsterdam. Here in the kibbutz she cannot paint. She has no room to paint, no canvas to paint on, no paint with which to paint. Maya walks through the kibbutz, past the children's house where she slept from age three months to thirteen, past the volunteer house, past the block of apartments where she moved after the children's house. All the houses and apartments are private now. The children's houses now occupied by Ethiopians airlifted to Israel in the early nineties.

She pulls down a ripe peach and eats it neatly. She throws the pit into the bushes and climbs the fence that surrounds the pool. She drags a cement block used in winter to hold the plastic pool cover in place. Maya fusses around with clothing and bits of rope that she ties tightly around her leg. She checks her knots. Then she turns off the iPod and sets it down on the grass. Let the last song played, the German punk song "Selbstmord Schlampe Hundchen," be her notification. The air is so dry it singes the inside of her mouth.

She launches herself into the pool. The rope slices tight into her ankle. A strong swimmer, she thrashes about. The cement block settles on the pool floor without dragging her under. The rope is too long and the pool is too shallow. Bad luck. Maya's bad luck. *What will we do about Maya?* She dives down to untie the knot but the water is too dark, too cold. The knot is too strong. She comes up, cold and tired and furious with herself.

Kobi Benjamin, walking along the road and smoking a joint, sees that someone is in the pool. He climbs the fence quickly. It might be a dog.

He does not touch Maya. The soft way he talks to her makes her weep a little. Once, when they were teenagers, he kissed her in the dining room. They were there to clean up after the Hanukkah party. It was empty. Marc, her boyfriend back then, had gone back to his room already. Does Kobi remember? It seems inconceivable that he has children, slow Kobi Benjamin. He dives in and hauls up the cement block and carries it to the side of the pool. She paddles after him and he cuts the rope with his pocketknife, setting her free.

Her attempt was one of a rash of suicides, Vivienne says out loud. She has just heard the story of Maya from Aliza next door. First, there was the boy who jumped from the silo. Then, the girl who set herself on fire outside the dining room. Another boy who killed himself on a moonlit night hunting boar. No one knew if it was an accident or not. And now Maya.

Yakov, in the next room, shouts to her over the television news. That is not a rash! Those suicides had ten years at least between them.

Vivienne wonders if Guy Gever will kill himself. He is a good shot. For years, not a night went by that trucks filled with Gever men and their cronies had not taken off into the valleys, near the ruins around Beit She'an, to shoot the wild birds.

And Keren wonders, who am I?

She walks and she wonders about the way she walks. How does her speech come out? How does an organic material, the weird flesh of the eyeball, allow her to see? When did her gait acquire this rhythm? This quality of sound as she pads across the tiled floor of the house that she and Guy have just remodeled.

She sits in the garden chair on her and Guy's patio and crosses her legs. The plastic of the chair bites into the back of her thigh. The neighborhood children play on the lawn. Her son is just returning from school. The boy who lives next door stands shyly off to the side of the children on the lawn not daring to join. Vivienne sits on the bench and watches Keren and Keren's friend Sagit, who joins them for a cup of Nescafé. Since the children are bigger now, Keren hasn't much use for her mother. Vivienne wishes to be her ally, her confidante. Like when Keren was a child and she helped Vivienne with her younger siblings.

The children beg for cartiv, Popsicles.

Keren's friend Sagit explains to Keren why she still breast-feeds her four-year-old and insists on carrying him around in a sling.

In Africa, Sagit says, the children's feet don't touch the ground until they are five years old.

So that's what I did wrong with my children, Keren says. Her lips grip like a vise onto the cigarette in her mouth. She has taken to smoking again. Is that what you mean?

Guy returns to the house that night. Keren sees the pickup truck approaching. She stiffens. Their two children mill around with their friends, kicking a soccer ball between them. When they see Guy, they brace themselves. Vivienne watches and waits. Men have always gone crazy. They are the more fragile sex. Even Yakov had his bad time when he found out about Ziv. Guy is clean and carrying flowers he picked from the neighbor's yard. The neighbor, Mrs. Benjamin, the Englishwoman, comes out shaking an umbrella and shouting in English. This makes them laugh. Mrs. Benjamin did three ulpans and still can't speak Hebrew. The Gevers know no English.

Guy gets down on one knee in front of Keren. The two Gever children and neighbor child edge away from him and Guy turns and shouts, Lech mi po! Get out of here! He rips the flowers, pulls the petals off the pretty stems and tears the bald heads off. He holds the petals in his hand. What a work of nature those petals are!

Abba, Yael says, you have to go. You're not well. You're frightening us. She is so beautiful, at eleven years old. She is the oldest. Born to Keren just nine months after she'd finished her army service.

Look, girl, Guy says, crossing the patio. This is my house. I'm not going anywhere. It's all of you who must leave. Only she can stay. He points at his mother-in-law, Vivienne. She's the only one who was ever nice to me! She is the only one who understands what it is to have an artistic soul.

Vivienne turns her face away and walks quickly off the porch and into the darkness.

Guy Gever screws up into a rage. He begins to shout. His son, Ari, tries to calm him. He is so small and helpless. Yael threatens to call the police.

Ima, the children cry.

Keren can't think. She grabs the children by their arms and hugs them close. She says, Everyone out, please go. Go to your savta Vivienne's house and she will make you dinner, she says to Yael. Take your brother. Everything will be calm. Don't worry.

Guy smirks at them as they leave. He grabs another handful of Mrs. Benjamin's petals from the cement of the patio and sprinkles them over each child's head as they pass. This, he says, is the blessing of the father.

Keren is shaking. Guy Gever grips her hand and leads her into the house to the bedroom. Keren sits on the bed. He hums a song, a love song from fifteen years ago, when they were young. We were going to try and have another baby, do you remember? he says. It is time, he says. Ari is already seven. Two children is not a proper family. Keren falls to the bed and moans, covering her face with her hands.

You must go, Guy Gever. You must go. You can't stay here and frighten everyone like this! You must go somewhere until you get well. Or you find yourself. Or whatever it is you need!

He freezes, hardens. Where will I go? I have no money. I have no job.

I don't know, she says. She looks up at him.

He sits on the bed beside her and considers it. You have to give me money, then. Money to eat. Money to create. Money for shovels and rakes. Perhaps a pair of gardening gloves. My hands are so rough now.

How much?

Eight hundred.

She's got twelve hundred shekels hidden away in the laundry room. Money she'd taken from the account two months ago when he'd started to spend so much of it. Before he'd quit his job in Beit She'an. She goes to the laundry room, returns, and hands the money to Guy Gever. He kisses her hard on the mouth, backs out the door. He rips up the bills, one by one by one, kicking them into Mrs. Benjamin's flower beds. The door closes with a bang. Who needs money? he says. The whole world is my canvas. Trees and shrubs are abundant. They are here for me to work with. I will take care of all of us. You don't believe me now but you wait and see.

Keren does not believe him.

Guy Gever is on the main road by the tree. He stacks the bushes he's ripped from the neighbor's patio one on top of the other. It is obvious to him, if to no one else, that they are sacred shrubs with a high spiritual vibration. They are the bushes his forefathers walked beside and prayed beside and they were longing to be freed from the earth. He will strap them to his back and take them to Moses who waits on the other side of the Red Sea. They will speak to him as they did to Moses. Their roots have been under the ground for so long, doing their dark work.

Maya heads out to the grove of pecan trees with her bag and her iPod. She walks through the wadi, along the path to the Yam Kinneret, the Sea of Galilee. She has walked this path so many times. The water bends the light of the moon. The peacocks howl in the night. She hears shotgun fire. Crazy Guy Gever and his hunting friends chasing poor animals through the fields. Shooting birds from the sky and rabbits in the ground. Nothing ever changes around here.

The trees lean down to her, caught in the wind. If she could grip the tip of one of them, it would launch her into the sky.

She swallows the tranquilizers and sits down heavily on the small rocks of the shore. She pulls off her sandals and stretches her legs until they meet the quiet water. She sees the lights of Tiberias across the sea. Soon she will get up and wade in. What to do about Maya? Maya will take care of herself, thank you very much.

Oh, the voice says, so you're giving yourself a little mikvah, is that it? The Ethiopians have set up a perfectly good one just down the hill, you know. It's very clean. They are devout, the little cushim. I hear they steal chlorine from the pool shed.

Hands reach under her arms and pull her away from the shore. She is dragged into brush, hidden from the shore and the path. Did you come all the way from Amsterdam to drown yourself? Have they no water in the Netherlands?

Maya had, in fact, once been baptized by born-again Christians. They'd dosed her with methadone, prayed over her in a caravan, and nearly drowned her in the Amstel.

Maya looks behind her to see Guy Gever, who turns a finger clockwise around his ear. We are the crazy ones in the kibbutz. You and I.

She shakes her head. She is nothing like Guy Gever.

You want something in you killed but you don't want killing it to kill you, yet you're willing to kill yourself in order to kill it if that's what it takes. Is that right?

Maya blinks at him.

That's no good, now is it? Life is heaped up full of disappointment. You have to be crazy enough to keep carrying one boulder up the hill after the other. To fill your pockets and the back of your truck with branches and sticks. To spend hours sweating in the sun making sculptures and then setting them on fire. Guy takes off his filthy shirt and dries her face with it. "And the dust returns to the earth as it was, and the spirit returns to God, who gave it." I dig up the dust and give the spirit back to God, but what you need, Maya, is an anchor. Guy Gever stands up and cuts the boughs of a pine, with the large hunting knife he keeps strapped to his leg. He lays the boughs down on the dry ground. Here you go, this will be soft-like. Lie down here and I'll show you what I'm talking about.

She lies on the ground while Guy Gever works. It is nice, finally, to have someone fuss over her. He builds a low wall the length of her body. I will be right back, he tells her. As he walks away, he wonders, Should I just shoot her? He has his pistol in the truck, under the seat. Should I just shoot her? He heard about all her problems in Amsterdam. Before his mother died, she was best friends with Maya's mother. Over the years, Guy has heard about Maya's drug addiction, abortions, and divorce. And worst of all for her mother: her brief conversion to Christianity.

Should I shoot her?

Maya lies on the soft boughs, near sleeping; her jeans are wet and cold on her skin. She half listens to the forest around her. It drones on above her.

Guy Gever returns. Glistening with sweat, he hoists a large, flat paver from his shoulders and sets it carefully on a pile of cement blocks, so that her body is only a third or so covered. The paver is warm. It retains heat from the sun. Don't want it to crush you, he says. I made that wall strong. You need to be anchored, otherwise you will fly up to the sky. You need to stay here and make your art, Guy says. Trust me, you want to stay here a little longer among the living. You will find your way. He laughs and disappears again. He returns again with another paver and sets this one over the top half of her body. He grunts as the paver settles on the blocks. Inside the tomb Guy has built, Maya is passed out and snoring.

Guy Gever stands a moment, swaying slightly over her. He has cared for her well. With his cell phone he dials the number for his uncle who mans the front gate. There is no answer so he leaves a message with Maya's whereabouts. Then walks away, scattering a handful of sunflower seeds and his cell phone into the sea.

Now who's crazy, Guy says. After all, only a maniac can stop time.

He knows the direction to go. Guy leaves his truck by the side of the wadi, and heads to Jordan, to the red rocks of Petra, on foot.

Chapter 2

In the Meantime

Guy Gever shuffles along the corridor of the new house. He is taking the medication the doctors have prescribed. They are trying to beat the art out of him. He knows. But he is trying to save his marriage. If he doesn't take his medication and go back to work, Keren says she will leave. The house they've built on the outskirts of the kibbutz costs just a little more per month than Keren can bring in and they are going to need the money. He will have to go back to work. They have debts from the renovations they did while he was working. His bank account is minus. She cannot ask her father for a loan. Guy forbids it.

He is fascinated by what registers with him and what escapes him. What escapes him is white and blank. What registers is pulpy like flesh, the sun streaming in through the living room window. He is walking into that light. Warmth on his arms. Since the army, he has never left Israel. Not even once. Not even to Sinai to hang out and smoke hashish with the Bedouin.

Keren breathes a sigh of relief. She's hidden the Xanax and she is waiting for that veil to lift. At least he's up and walking around. Her mother, Vivienne, looks away. Mon Dieu, she says. I've just made ktsitsot, Vivienne says, meatballs made from the wild boar the kibbutzniks shot the night before. Would you like some, motek?

The doctors tell her he shouldn't have such a strong reaction to the medication, but they've already spent years trying to adjust it. She would like to take him to a private doctor but it costs a fortune. She would like to borrow money from her father for this, but Guy says no. He refuses to take money from anyone.

The rabbi Yoni Keret, who lives in the metal caravans on the outskirts of the kibbutz, says this madness is God's curative for Guy Gever's once wayward ways. The rabbi uses words like "palliative" and "tonic." Prayer will wash him clean, the rabbi says. Yoni Keret thrusts prayer books into Guy's hands. Guy steals money from Keren's bag and gives it to Yoni Keret, who gives the money to the poor children of the men who pray in Jerusalem. This irritates Keren. Those poor religious children wouldn't be so impoverished if their fathers stopped praying and went to work. They wouldn't be so poor if their mothers stopped having babies. But it makes Guy happy. It soothes him to imagine God is looking down on him, smiling at him for his good deeds.

If he becomes religious on top of everything else, Keren will leave him.

Guy Gever wears workman's trousers, the kind the men in the kibbutz wear to muck out the chicken house, and they are held up with a rope tied in a knot. She has never seen him wear such clothing. He has always been neatly dressed, even dapper. Guy clumsily attempts to untie the knot. Because of his medication, he has balance issues. He has constipation issues. He is impotent.

Keren grows older. Soon she will dry up like a grape. She won't want to have sex at all. But that it does not bother Guy bothers Keren the most. She has heard that lack of desire is a side effect of medication, but how can he not care for sex? They'd thought once of having a large family. It seems that won't happen now.

Keren goes to the Druze village and has a woman concoct a tea for Guy, to bring carnal thoughts back into his head. She hopes it will give him rational thoughts again and bring him back to her. Even if he cannot perform in any meaningful way, Keren would like to feel Guy's hands around her waist, his mouth buried in her neck. For him to grab her ass, put his hand under her shirt. She is still young, still in good shape, exercises regularly, and takes aerobics classes at the community center. The children are more or less self-sufficient in the kibbutz. There are many bubbes and savtot watching out for them.

Vivienne sits in the Gever living room with a magazine open on her lap. She purses her lips and tries to think of something to say that won't offend her daughter. Keren is hyperalert and lies in wait for any sort of stinging comment from her mother. Lately Vivienne has been trying hard to watch what she says. As a result, she hardly speaks anymore. The magazine beckons.

An Israeli model is dating a big Hollywood movie star. There is a picture of them on the movie star's yacht.

Guy no longer has energy to hunt at night. He almost never leaves the house.

Keren eyes her husband. It is Shabbat evening in April. He lies on the old couch with his back to her. He is like a child, Guy Gever. But wasn't he always? And isn't that why Keren loved him in the first place?

Keren had always secretly believed him, believed that the Gevers were special in the kibbutz. Touched by God. Maybe God or the prophets or the cypress and eucalyptus trees in the fields or the birds or that mad girl who'd nearly killed herself. He'd saved that girl, Guy Gever had, all those years ago. Her little brother's ex-girlfriend. What was her name? It was like it was meant to be. Keren talks unconsciously to her mother, not expecting a response, almost like she is talking to herself.

Vivienne Solomon rolls her eyes when she hears things like this. It reminds her of the superstitions of the old country. In Algeria, there had always been two sets of dishes and two iceboxes to keep kosher. There was a prayer for every activity and scarves over her mother's pretty hair. It reminds her of the nuns in the French school she attended as a girl. With Jesus nailed to the cross, their hand gestures, their Marie de grêle. This is why she had come to the kibbutz, a Zionist. Communism had called her. So maybe it hadn't worked so well and maybe she should have gone to France instead. The kibbutzim collapsing all throughout Israel, bankrupt and squabbling for what little resources had not already been squandered away by laziness and ill-management. But never had she thought the datiyim, the religious with their black hats and curls around their faces, would come to the kibbutz. The kibbutz! Where Yakov himself had famously eaten pork sausage on Yom Kippur! Now, the datiyim sit in their caravans and try to recruit the young kids newly returned from India, all turned around on drugs and spiritual nonsense. Those kids, the ruined and the damned, are the ones the datiyim want. But what the rabbi wants with Guy Gever is anyone's guess.

Guy Gever shuffles off and Keren sits beside Vivienne on the sofa. She rests her hand on her mother's knee and says, He is worse since taking that medication. Now he really seems crazy.

Vivienne closes her eyes and nods. You are right, Vivienne says. Get him off the medication. We will find something for him to do. Al tidagi, Vivienne says. Do not worry.

Keren thinks of taking time off work. She will take him someplace quiet. Maybe Cyprus. Maybe Eilat. And she will wean him from the medicine that has stolen Guy Gever from her. She will restore him. Together they will find their way again. If not for them, then for the children and their future children.

Chapter 3

THE PACIFIC

THE THING to do when your house is being searched, your husband arrested, and your bank accounts seized is to procure large amounts of Xanax. Dip into hidden reserves. Borrow from your neighbors. High-quality painkillers are even better. There is codeine. Percocet or Darvocet. The ultimate is oxycodone. If you have the will and the connections there are also street drugs that can send you into the oblivion you crave.

You are not paranoid. Your house, in fact, is bugged.

Avoid marijuana.

You've seen the wives on the news. They stand beside their husbands, guilty husbands and husbands falsely accused. The women, stony, glassy-eyed. A lip trembles. Behind that pharmaceutical veneer is someone ready to bolt, if not for the children she is shackled to.

Carolyn lives with her family in Santa Monica, not far from the ocean. They moved five years ago from Connecticut. In the summer, the roads fill with cheery beachgoers and surfers. Carolyn walks her dogs along the beach before noon. She meets others like her. Their dogs walked on leashes. Their children tucked away in schools. There are waves and sunlight and gulls that lift the sunlight, and cast tracks and seagull shit across the beaches that run down to the sea. Coyotes come from the Santa Monica Mountains and ferret through garbage cans.

Carolyn sends the children off to school on the bus and settles back into bed with a mug of coffee and a to-do list. Often what she does these days, since she left her job, is read magazines and news and gossip on the Internet. Carolyn flips through cable channels. She clips her toenails. She thinks about going downtown and taking a yoga class.

Downstairs, someone bangs on the front door. The dogs bark. FedEx or UPS, probably. She runs down the stairs, pulling a cardigan over her camisole. The banging grows louder and more insistent. The dogs are falling all over one another. She shoos them away and opens the front door. A dozen or so men push into her house. They say, We are the LAPD. We have a search warrant. Your husband, Marc Solomon, and his business partner have been arrested.

The stream of their words hits her with the full force of a fire hose: Your house is now a crime scene. You must sit on the couch here in the living room. You must not get up. Would you like a glass of water?

The men open cabinets. They circle around the rattan table in the great room. They pick it up and set it down. Its glass top slides to the floor. They look up at her with sheepish expressions. They inspect the base of the table, searching it for a hidden safe. They are searching for drugs or diamonds. Money or meth labs. Perhaps they are looking for missing limbs and stolen organs. She has never read mystery novels. She doesn't watch crime shows on television.

She is the daughter of schoolteachers. Her father is an art history professor in the Midwest. Her mother has died. Why has no one prepared her for this moment?

Carolyn thinks about walking into the cold water of the Pacific Ocean, fully clothed. Perhaps she would wear her husband's heavy trench coat and his heaviest watch. She turns around and surveys her green lawn. Green in spite of the drought. Their water bills are astronomical. But it is raining now. When they release her and leave her house she will have no choice but to try and swim across the ocean until she reaches the islands. The lights of the Pacific Ocean will guide her, their soft white waves undulating. Through the mist, Carolyn sees a green light shining off the pier, or a boat. She has long been fascinated by women who swim across large, cold bodies of water. There was once a woman who swam all the way from Cuba to Miami. Why would they do this except to save their lives?

She has heard drowning is painful.

The chief detective holds her arm and walks her down the hallway. She is led to the bed and the detective sits on a chair across from her. He turns on a small lamp. The rain sluices down the windows and everything outside is wet concrete-gray. The ocean roils. A newspaper thuds onto the porch.

He says, We know you know what's going on and what your husband has been up to. And, you realize, we've been good to you in spite of your criminal activity. You realize, by withholding information you are committing a crime.

Yes. But I am not withholding information.

He reaches over and holds her arm, pinching it gently at the elbow. His fingers are small and delicate. He says, We haven't torn up your house. We waited until your children left for school.

She nods.

So now you have to tell me where the safe is. You have to tell me where the guns are and if there are drugs. If we find out you've been lying to us, if we find something you haven't told us about, someone else will have to pick up your children. Not you. Do you understand?

The house and its objects. A vibrator in an upstairs drawer, a messy linen closet, email flirtations, nude photos, even a video. The spice cabinet is a mess. Some paprika spilled, there is rank orange powder all over the shelves. She has been meaning to get to it. There is probably a joint somewhere. An abandoned canvas and dried-up paints in a spare room. She used to smoke a little and watch the water on summer nights with Marc after the children had gone to bed. Where is the Xanax? Other secrets.

She shakes her head. No guns. No safe. No drugs.

Her teeth chatter.

She says, I know every inch of this house. I haven't been in the attic recently. But you were just there. Did you find anything?

She tries to remember what's in the attic. Children's clothing and artwork. Summer things. Old, moldy camping gear from her childhood. College textbooks. Her husband's dress uniform. The medals in a plastic bag tucked into a pocket of the jacket.

The bottle of Xanax in her bedside table drawer.

He lets go of her arm and stares at her for a long while. She stares back. Another man walks into the bedroom and the two leave together. She sits very still on the edge of the bed. It is colder in the bedroom than in the living room.

Should she let her teeth chatter? Should she try to stop them from chattering?

She wills her teeth to stop chattering.

She tells herself: This is how you act when the police are searching your house.

One of the detectives sees her still perched on the bed. Need something? he asks. Glass of water? No? You can go back to the living room.

From the couch she watches the LA County detectives pick up the rattan table again and again. They remove the glass top and lean it up against the sofa. They flip the table over again and reexamine it. They knock on the table to see if it is hollow. She wonders if they will take a knife to it. Or bludgeon it. Or bludgeon her. The detectives blur together. She can't tell them apart.

A cop stands beside the fireplace in his uniform. He is local and friendly. He asks her if she's gone to the new breakfast place in Santa Monica. He tells her she has a nice house and a nice view. She probably pays a lot of property taxes, right? He asks her how many square feet the house is. He asks which school her children go to. He asks if she likes the schools. He asks if the rug on the floor was expensive. He asks if she likes to shop and where. This area is rich, he says. Takes a lot of money to live here. Me, I live in the Valley.

Again, they tell her how nice they are. They write down everything they take. Computers, laptops, tablets, and old cell phones are gathered in a heap in the foyer. There will be an inventory list to sign off on before they go.

Scenarios play out in her head. Where will they go, how will she support herself, what will the neighbors think? Her next-door neighbor who heads out every Sunday morning in her late model Cadillac presumably dressed for church. What will she think?

The heavy dogs mill around her feet.

The rain stops. Early March. The street holds a cool mist. A wind from the sea sweeps up and blows the mist away. Seven unmarked cars lined up along the front yard. The last is a Santa Monica police car. The neighbor's Cadillac parked next door in the driveway.

The nanny will have to go.

They will have to cancel their memberships.

The children.

She turns back to the window and looks out at the street. Carolyn's neighbor walks her dog past their house. The dog sniffs at their bushes. Carolyn's dogs bark in response. The neighbor's face turns up toward her window. Her eyes meet Carolyn's. The neighbor gives her a slight wave.

Carolyn's mouth is dry. She smells bad. Gamey, like fear.

* * *

The detective stalks around the house. He grows more frustrated with each pass through the living room. He talks on his cell phone. He whispers to the other men. He wears slightly baggy but otherwise well-cut jeans and heavy, black shoes. When he sits, his jeans hitch up and show white athletic socks. He wears a black T-shirt that stretches across well-defined muscles. He is short. He has a goatee. His black hair thins out on top and she can see obscene flashes of his naked skull.

He sits on the couch. Tell me. When will your kids be coming home?

The youngest two at three, the oldest at four.

I don't want to have to tear your house apart, he says. We don't want to be here when your kids get back. You have to tell me the truth.

I could never lie to you, she says, like a lover accused of infidelity.

The detective fidgets. His foot jiggles on his knee. He has an Italian name, like Gambello or Gambini. She didn't catch it when he said it. He says, I believe you. You're a good woman. He pats her knee. I know you don't know what's going on. I see you're not involved in the things your husband is mixed up in. He says, Tell me, Carolyn Solomon, are you Catholic?

Yes, she lies.

A policeman comes to her holding a cell phone. She lifts it to her ear. It smells of his cologne.

On the line her husband says, It will be all right. Tell them everything. We've done nothing illegal and we have nothing to hide. It's a mistake, Marc says. A misunderstanding. The lawyers will handle everything.

The police and detectives stand around her.

When are you coming home? she asks.

I don't know, he says.

They said they have arrested your partner—

We never said that, says the detective.

Never mind, Marc says. It will be all right. My lawyers are here. It's just a misunderstanding. The detective takes the phone from her.

I love you, she says to the phone in the detective's hand.

They leave one by one. The last to go is the goateed detective who tells her to stay put. Pick up your children. Don't leave the house. Don't make any phone calls. Do you know what I'm saying?

I have no idea what you're saying.

His eyes are bored. Already conceiving his next case. Don't leave the house, he repeats. Don't call anyone. Don't talk to anyone.

Then the house is silent.

So much of what had happened had been coded, encrypted. She hadn't understood anything. It is a language no one had taught her. She has no working landline. The police have taken her phone. Carolyn heads out the front door and cuts through the hedge to the neighbor's house. Before she can knock, the door opens. Her neighbor eyes Carolyn from behind a crack in the door. I know what this is all about, she says to Carolyn. Your husband is running a big gambling ring out of that fancy LA office of his. Those LAPD officers got the search warrant from the village hall. I know because Mrs. Gregory told me. I called to ask her what was going on over at your house. She works there half-days.

Can I use your phone? Carolyn asks.

You know, she says. It's not that I don't like you. You and your kids. Those boys playing basketball until too late at night and your goddamned ostentatious *catered* parties. Your husband goes to work every morning in his fancy sports car. You're not from these parts. This used to be a small town, years and years ago, believe it or not, before you and your element moved here. I have lived here since 1955. Your husband is a foreigner. You don't know anything about this community. The old coastline. You never lock your front door.

How do you know I never lock my door?

I checked.

Could I have a glass of water?

Yes, she says. You may.

I'm not a foreigner, Carolyn says. I was born in Ohio.

Carolyn follows her into the living room and sits down on a low leather couch. She is spry and moves easily but she is much older than Carolyn had thought. The neighbor brings her water in a paper Dixie cup. I'll make you a cup of tea, she says. She is barefoot and her gnarled, veiny feet plunge into beige shag carpeting. She wears a robe over a jogging suit. Her hair, which is usually pulled back and severe, hangs gray and long around her face. She has beautiful hair.

The teakettle goes off and the neighbor walks to the kitchen. Carolyn hears a cabinet door open and shut. The furniture is old but the house is decorated tastefully. For a moment Carolyn imagines they become best friends. She adopts Carolyn and takes her and the children in after they've lost everything. The neighbor calls from the kitchen: Guess you don't mind what kind of tea I give you.

No, Carolyn says. I don't mind. She thinks to herself, so fiercely it's as though she's said it aloud: I have no mother.

The neighbor, who Carolyn remembers is named Grace, walks back into the living room and hands her the tea. Carolyn realizes again the rawness of Carolyn. She smells bad.

She asks Grace if she has a husband.

She has.

Was he there now?

Grace shakes her head no.

Carolyn tries to remember if she's ever seen a man in or around the house. The Solomons' house is new construction and bigger than all the neighbors' on the block. When the Solomons had first moved in they'd built a high fence between the properties.

Carolyn asks if she could use the bathroom and she is led through the living room. On the walls are bright matte paintings of sunbursts and spheres. The house is immaculate. There is a stack of *Christian Science Monitors* fanned out on the coffee table. They date back twenty years or more.

In the bathroom, the door shut and locked behind her, Carolyn opens the medicine cabinet. Inside is an old bottle of Secret. She removes the cap and inhales. It brings back her mother, dead now two years. There is a prescription bottle of antibiotics, a bottle of aspirin. An ancient box of Alka-Seltzer.

Carolyn shuts the medicine cabinet and flushes the toilet. She washes her hands and brings a limp, gray bar of soap to her armpits. She swipes the bar under her arms.

Shall I watch the children when they come home? Grace asks her.

No, Carolyn says. Thank you.

They sit together until her tea is finished. Carolyn uses Grace's phone to call Marc's cell phone. Every call goes straight to voice mail. She knows no one else's number by heart. She thinks about calling her father. She thinks about calling Marc's father, Yakov, and decides against it. Marc will be furious if she tells his father.

Carolyn stands up. Thank you, she says, and heads toward the front door. As Carolyn turns to say goodbye, Grace takes hold of both Carolyn's hands, opening her palms. Grace's hands are soft and warm.

What is not in your hands, she says, you don't have. She unlocks the dead bolt and the chain. Everything will be all right, she says. Remember. There are no bad people in the world. Only dark and stupid forces. You're a good person, Carolyn Solomon.

Carolyn wanders through the rooms of her house. For the most part everything is unharmed. Only the clothing in the closets is askew. Boxes of outgrown clothing have been upended. Toys strewn through the children's rooms. DVDs scattered.

They'd searched in the old iron baseboard heaters, tearing off the pieces on the ends and reaching in. Their fingers inched toward the cash, guns, and drugs they knew they'd find. If only they searched hard enough. In fact, in the end, none of it will matter and they could care less what was really found, or even if the allegations they'd made were true. What they wanted they had already: the contents of the bank accounts, some jewelry. A Rolex. The business accounts. Guilty or innocent, it didn't matter. They had their money.

They'd found condoms and scattered them across the floor of Marc's office.

While the police were there, nothing worse could happen to her. There was something paternal in their bullying tone. Now she sat with thoughts that were hard. She would have to sit alone until the children came.

They would come home on the bus and expect dinner to be made and require help with their homework. Carolyn would listen with cheerful impartiality to all their stories of friends and teachers, malevolent, benevolent, and otherwise. By bedtime they would wonder where their father had gone. He was always home by bedtime.

Chapter 4

IMALEH

JOSEPH CLIMBS the crumbling cement stairs to the apartment building on Hatsfira Street in the Moshava Germanit, the German Colony neighborhood of Jerusalem. His bag is heavy with homework, his soccer cleats and ball. He is not supposed to be staying there. He is supposed to be at his father's house, only his father is not really his father. Or so his older cousins tell him. He has spent the afternoon with his best friend, Mattan, but Mattan's mother is serving dinner now and he probably should be running along home.

Joseph unlocks the door and opens it. The smell of his mother fills his head. She left that morning to go to America on vacation. Imaleh, he says, to the silent rooms. Joseph shuts the door and locks it fast.

He is not afraid.

Joseph switches on the desktop in the kitchen. He watches YouTube videos, checks email, and launches Minecraft. In Minecraft, Joseph builds a pyramid and then destroys it. Zombies come and eat his pigs. Mattan's avatar pops up on the screen.

Together they build a farm. His crops are destroyed. It rains. They build a shelter and a bed. In the world of Minecraft, night comes and eight minutes later the sun rises. He tries survival mode but it's too difficult to survive for more than a few minutes. Zombies kill him. He drowns in lava. A pig mauls him. He prefers creator mode. In creator mode anything can happen. You can teleport. You can fly. Mattan signs out. It should be bath time for him. But Joseph can do whatever he likes.

Joseph shuts down Minecraft and sends his ima an email and also one to his cousin Izaac in America. In the emails he asks them not to forget to send the Lego. *Please*, he writes in English, *don't forget. Tell my mom.*

Joseph is eleven years old. Almost twelve.

There is a Minecraft Lego he wants very much.

He finishes his homework. He works especially hard in English.

Joseph would like to go to the US and live in his cousin Izaac's house. Izaac has a real, almost-American father, Dod Marc, who lives in the same house with them. Marc plays basketball with Izaac, swims with Izaac, goes on bike rides with Izaac. Izaac also has two proper younger brothers. Not half-siblings. *Real* siblings. Their house in America is enormous. It is right on the beach. A mansion somewhere close to Hollywood. They have two dogs. Dod Marc drives a tiny sports car to his office in downtown Los Angeles. His cousins have never ridden on a bus or train in their whole lives. Once when Dod Marc came to Israel, Izaac and Joseph watched him play cadoor regel with all the other dads. In America, they call this soccer. Marc had once been the best cadoor regel player in all of the Jordan Valley. If he had not been in Shayetet 13 he would have joined Beitar Jerusalem or maybe even Manchester United. Everyone in the kibbutz says Joseph looks and acts just like his Dod Marc. He looks more like Marc than Izaac does. He has the same ball-handling skills. Now, Marc is slow and out of shape. His belly is a little heavy. The older men had stood around and laughed at Marc when he played in the kibbutz. He has too much money in his pockets, the men said. It weighs him down, all those American dollars.

Math is hard. Joseph knows if he fudges the numbers, his teacher will never check closely. He writes the answers in faintly with pencil so that he may erase them and fill in the correct answers when the class goes over their work. He has read all of Harry Potter. His mother even had a small part in the fourth Harry Potter movie.

Joseph is a good student. He reads constantly. I was not a good student, his mother says. I always hated to read. He must be like his father, she says.

Joseph is not sure which father she means. Is it Abba who lives in the Old City with his new wife and baby? Or the fat man on the Internet his cousins show him when they want to tease.

Which is it, Ima?

His best friend, Mattan, says, Don't be an idiot. Your father is your father. Don't listen to your cousins' stupid stories. You look just like Lior, Mattan says. Lior is his cousin on his father's side and he goes to school with Mattan and Joseph.

This is true, Joseph agrees. In some photos he looks just like Lior.

By eight p.m. he is starving. He calls the Italian restaurant down the street and orders pasta Bolognese and fries and a can of Coca-Cola. He uses his Saba Yakov's credit card to pay. It is to be used only in emergencies but this is an emergency as Joseph is very hungry. There is no one to cook for him. His father's house is not an option. He doesn't really seem to want Joseph around and it's only for a week and Joseph figures he can go it alone. He is very independent.

But he is not used to being alone. When his mother works, she usually hires the nice student who lives down the street to watch him. The student is a beautiful yoga teacher studying at Hebrew University and Joseph is a little bit in love with her. Joseph should be staying with his father, only it seems his father has forgotten. He was not there to pick Joseph up from school as he should have been. Anyway, at Abba's house, there is no cable television, the new baby cries every second, the twin toddlers get into his things, and the new wife hates him. There are too many people crammed into the small apartment so Joseph has to sleep on the couch. Plus his stepmother never lets Joseph on her computer. He would die of boredom.

Also, he has heard from his cousins in the kibbutz that the Old City where his father lives is full of Arabs and that Arabs eat Jewish children, and cats.

The food arrives. Mohammed, the deliveryman, high-fives Joseph. Joseph gives him a five-shekel coin for a tip. This is too much, the deliveryman says. The deliveryman gives Joseph one shekel back.

You are one of the good ones, Mohammed says.

Ayelet and Shira are both actors but Ayelet earns most of her living the old-fashioned way: a wealthy husband. They met in their early twenties when they starred together in an Israeli sitcom based on the British show *Coupling*. Shira invested most of her earnings, which at the time were substantial, with her brother Marc's help, and has been living off the investments ever since. Ayelet married a rich tech guy and is the host of the Israeli *Survivor*. The Moshava where they live is packed with wealthy hipsters. New restaurants open weekly. Rents and housing costs have skyrocketed. Residents have banded together to stop incoming hotels and high-rises. Shira was lucky enough to secure her apartment when prices were low and now pays two hundred shekels a month, or about fifty dollars in a setup similar to rent control. She can never sell it. She can never pass it on to her children, but she can live there forever for about the price of one cappuccino a day. One day, when she makes it big, she'll buy a place in Tel Aviv, in Yaffo or Shenkin, but for now she stays and travels to Tel Aviv for work. Cats in Jerusalem slink and shit and mate around mansions that are now worth millions of shekels and are being snapped up by Russian billionaires and French millionaires. Shira's friends are socialists and communists and peaceniks. They send their children to bilingual schools with Arab children and schools that practice progressive education curricula. They pick olives with Palestinians and smuggle Palestinian women to Tel Aviv beaches by dressing them in trendy Israeli clothing. They eat bio, that is, organic food and wear pants with crotches that reach down to their knees.

On Shabbat afternoons, they ride on old-fashioned bicycles to their Pilates studios and cafés. They practice the Alexander Technique. They do Feldenkrais. They do Avi Grinberg. They are shipwrecked on the coast of the Israeli left.

Shira is Joseph's mother.

Shira was once the sort of tiny, thirty-something-year-old woman who looked prepubescent. But lately, Shira has grown quite fat. She has been eating far too much pitot and falafelim, tststot ve burekasim. She has not had enough regular work to justify the starvation necessary to maintain "camera weight." She'd had her breasts done recently with the money she received from a movie she did for the HOT cable network. All the soldiers in her brother Ziv's special forces unit had once salivated over her. She'd blown them all, one by one by one, during a period of her life her therapist describes as *giving all her power away.*

Shira's trip to Los Angeles is a vacation from the summer movement protesting high rents in Israel. She had traveled especially to Tel Aviv with her boyfriend Asaf Boulboulim. The movement was founded by him, and is supported by Shira and Ayelet and their actor and producer friends. Asaf has been living with Shira in the Moshava to save money for his movement.

Asaf Boulboulim is a Zen Buddhist peace activist. He is a dropout of Bezalel Academy where he had studied sculpture. He stands on street corners and passes out flyers that say, *The world is an illusion. No separation between culture and race and religion. We are all one. We are cousins. We are our brothers' keepers.* Asaf tells Shira that the next industrial revolution will be robots acting as worker bees and we will all be queens. There will be no need for money so there will be no wars. There will be true equality between Jews and Arabs.

Asaf and Shira have tried all the new restaurants in Jerusalem together. They order food in from the Italian restaurant and have it delivered. They regularly take the train to Tel Aviv when Joseph is with his father for protests, parties, film premieres, and restaurant openings. Shira has nearly drained her bank account. He tells her that this is all right. Soon money will be obsolete anyway. She is an actor who enjoys the work she does. It is okay for her to keep working. In fact, when she returns from LA, he thinks she should find another job. Asaf thinks Shira should perhaps look for work during the week she's in LA. They will need more money than just her investments for his movement. Perhaps he will also be an actor. He wonders if maybe Shira can help him find acting jobs.

Shira's father, Yakov Solomon, refuses to meet him. Asaf is too young for Shira. He is not a good influence. He is not serious. She should find a working man, a businessman, a laborer. Any man but this man who lives in Shira's house and pays for nothing. Asaf Boulboulim is useless, a parasite.

Yakov Solomon, according to Asaf Boulboulim, is immoral for making so much money in construction when construction creates separation between people, when Yakov—a communist in the kibbutz!—had once believed in the ideals of the common man. Asaf's highest aspiration is to be an anarchist. A Buddhist anarchist like Milarepa, a trickster, a jackal.

It is difficult for Shira to explain to her father that an anarchist is more chic than a nihilist, a capitalist, or the communists of the kibbutz where Shira Solomon was raised. But in truth, Shira doesn't care at all for politics. All she cares for is love and art.

When Shira and Ayelet are not working, they like to sit in cafés and smoke cigarettes. They order endless cups of milky café hafuch. Their hair is long and dyed black as night and hangs nearly to their waists. In certain clothing, from certain angles, Shira still looks thin. She wears low-cut shirts to show off her breasts. She never wears a bra. She enjoys the way her nipples poke out of the shirt fabric, high and firm. She always wears Spanx in public. When she wears Spanx, she eats less.

Shira and Ayelet fly into the shithole that is LAX airport. Shira's brother Marc picks them up in his sporty BMW. It takes two hours to maneuver the highways. He drives them into West Hollywood where they will stay at the Standard Hotel on Sunset. They were able to find a room there for one hundred fifty dollars a night.

Shira sits in front next to Marc. Ayelet sits crammed in the back and rattles off the names of stores they'd like to see: Uniqlo, J. Crew, Madewell, Lululemon, and Barneys. Most stores are in the Grove off Fairfax. Everything is so much cheaper in America, Shira says. And better quality, says Ayelet. Shira tells Marc she would love to come visit Carolyn and the kids in Santa Monica. When is a good time? Her rapid speech is fueled by exhaustion, by adrenaline, by excitement. She turns in her seat and addresses Ayelet, who blinks sleepily at her. Ayelet's head falls against the seat and she exhales loudly. Ayelet is still so small, like a doll in the tiny backseat of the car. She opens her eyes. Beseder, Ayelet sighs. When will we be there?

Marc drives the car expertly through the traffic. There's nothing to light the eyes on but the occasional palm tree and the cement walls of the expressway. Graffiti. Until they get close to the Standard on Sunset, there will be nothing, thinks Shira, just pretty Ayelet in the back and her handsome brother Marc beside her. He still has all his hair and barely a gray one. He looks fit and young.

Shira thinks of Joseph, how he would like to be here in LA with her. His eyes would shine with excitement and he would chatter nonstop. They would go to Disneyland and Universal Studios. He loves to visit America, to visit his cousins and his Dod Marc. Her chest constricts. But she'd wanted a girl's vacation. A break, a treat, something just for Shira. She hopes he is happy at his father's house. He is an optimistic child, and adaptable. He will be all right.

Marc Solomon pulls into the Standard. Shira had stayed there twelve years ago when she appeared in her first American film. She'd fucked an entire band from Liverpool on the blue AstroTurf around the pool. She wonders if there is still AstroTurf around the pool. Marc shows them the Uber app and promises to visit and take them out to lunch. He carries their nearly empty suitcases through the door to the lobby. He's got to go. He's got work to do.

I'll come visit you and Carolyn and the kids, Shira says, as Marc walks to the door.

Don't trouble yourself, Marc says. We'll see you in haaretz in a few months, for the holidays. Enjoy yourself.

Ayelet has a friend who sells hash in Silver Lake. This friend brings them a small bag and Ayelet pays. The friend is an Israeli savta, quite round, with flowing skirts, a friend of Ayelet's mother, who was also a folk singer from the sixties. Rumor had it the savta had an affair with Bob Dylan back in the old days. She annoys Shira when she sits down on the sofa to smoke with Ayelet. The Standard room is nonsmoking. Shira wishes they would go out to the terrace, or maybe to the savta's house in Silver Lake. Ayelet says she plans to smoke just a little bit of the marijuana. A little bit each and every day. Perhaps once when they first wake up, once in the afternoon, and maybe just a little at night before a bath. It is so pleasurable—Ayelet exhales a fragrant cloud—to smoke pot in the bathtub. Shira smokes too although she's never liked it much. It makes her paranoid.

An hour after the savta leaves, Marc's wife, annoying, American, comes to greet them and say hello. I was taking a yoga class, Carolyn says, right off Sunset. A great studio. Shira tries to smile but she hates yoga. Carolyn hands Shira a present, a small bag of See's chocolate, and smiles in that American way where gratitude is expected. Carolyn has also gained weight and she's too blond. Almost platinum. She's straightened her naturally curly hair into a curtain of white-blond.

Carolyn asks Shira if it isn't difficult leaving her son for so many days. Carolyn herself has never left her children for that many days in a row.

It is good for him to be with his father, Shira says. It is good for him to bond with his new baby brother and the twins.

Carolyn shows them which direction the Grove is. She offers them a ride. She tells them no one in LA walks anywhere. Are they sure they wouldn't like a ride? Carolyn points out the no-smoking sign in the room. You'll get fined if you smoke, Carolyn says, pointing at the American Spirits they've tossed onto the dresser. And anyway, it's not very healthy. Do people still smoke so much in Israel?

Who is watching the boys? Shira asks.

Carolyn smiles tightly. They are watching themselves.

Together they have a list of stores to find and a map. They open their computers and send emails and check Facebook statuses. Shira sends Joseph an email. She thinks to call him at his father's, but she will have to purchase a phone card. She will try to remember to do that tomorrow. They roll another joint. They add tobacco from the American Spirit cigarettes. They shower and dress in fresh clothing. They apply lipstick. Ayelet marks on the map the stores on their list.

Shira takes her bag into the bathroom. She sits on the toilet and pees. She doesn't want to spend too much money. She keeps to a strict allowance she has set for herself most weeks, but Asaf has been requesting more and more money for his causes.

Ayelet dozes on the sofa. Motek, she says with half-closed eyes, here we are in Los Angeles, California.

The city of angels, Shira says.

There are noises out in the hallway. A shriek and a laugh from neighbors or thieves or rapists. The light has changed outside. Their patio door opens onto the blue AstroTurf of the pool. Suddenly everything looks seedy and sinister. This is Los Angeles and they are two young and attractive women. They are quite stoned. They discuss whether to stay inside or venture out. They decide they are too tired and too stoned to leave anyway. It is four o'clock in the afternoon Los Angeles time when Ayelet falls asleep, sitting up on the couch, her mouth falling open and revealing her bucked teeth, the only thing about Ayelet that isn't pretty.

Shira checks emails on her laptop and sends one to Joseph, who has said he is very happy but misses her. He reminds her of the Lego he wants. The Minecraft one.

She misses Joseph so much she feels an acute pain in the bone between her breasts. She clutches at her throat and quells maternal panic, thinking: He is better there. With his father, the new wife, siblings. A real family. She thinks of Carolyn's comment, about never leaving her children.

That bitch, Shira thinks.

Joseph finishes his schnitzel from the brasserie and dumps the greasy paper and packaging into the garbage. It has been three days since his mother left, and the garbage is piling up and beginning to smell bad. The sun streams into the kitchen. There are ants on the counter going after crumbs.

The phone rings and Joseph runs to pick it up.

Allo! Yakov Solomon shouts into the phone. Saba Yakov is hard of hearing.

Hello, Saba.

Tell me, yeled. Where is your mother?

She is in America, Saba. Don't you remember?

Remember? Of course I remember! I want to see what you know! When is she coming back?

I don't know. She said she was coming back yesterday or maybe tomorrow. I don't know.

Unexpectedly tears come to Joseph's eyes. Saba does not ask why Joseph is there alone.

You eating good? Yakov Solomon asks.

Yes.

Good! Tell your mother to call me when she gets back. Be good. Don't let the lions eat you.

Okay, Saba.

You know, I once *killed* a bear! I grabbed him by the ears with my bare hands and—

Yes. You told me that.

You're a good boy. You know that?

Yes, Saba.

You know who's bad?

Who, Saba?

The dogs are bad! For not eating you! Goodbye, yeled!

Bye, Saba.

Joseph hears in the distance the call to prayer.

He spends the next several hours creating a battleship out of his bunk bed and blankets, eating potato chips and cookies straight from their bags, and typing English words like "breast" and "vagina" into Google to see what comes up. He watches a soccer game on television. Liverpool against Madrid.

At eleven, he locks the terrace door. He double-checks the front door of the apartment.

Joseph climbs into his top bunk and reflects on his situation. Maybe it is dangerous to stay alone in an apartment when you are only eleven years old.

But then again, this is not America.

Shira grows bored with Ayelet in the hotel room. It's full of shopping bags. They've spent three days running up and down Melrose. They try on all their clothing in front of the mirror on the back of the bedroom door.

In three days, they are due to leave, back to Jerusalem. What will they do in the meantime?

Shira has a flash of understanding. She is in a constant state of wanting. Shira wants what she wants and she buys it. She takes it back to the hotel, a dress, a shirt, a bag, everything bought on sale. A great bargain. The relief from the wanting wears off the moment the garment hits the floor, discarded. On to the next!

Is there something Shira could buy that would eradicate all the wanting? That is the thing she wants most of all, whatever it is.

Ayelet produces a tiny bag of cocaine she bought from a salesman at Barneys.

They snort the cocaine on Ayelet's pocket mirror. This revives Ayelet for an hour or so. She tells Shira she is fucking her veterinarian and that they fuck on the examining table.

Ayelet, that is disgusting.

Ayelet blinks back at her. She nods her head slowly and says in a rush, You are right, of course, it *is* disgusting.

How is the sex? Shira asks.

Fantastic. Ayelet sinks into the couch, the mirror balanced on her lap. Fantastic.

Ayelet switches back to marijuana and turns on the television. Ayelet watches all the new episodes of *Weeds, Californication,* as well as *Game of Thrones* and *Destiny,* a show that was big in Israel and has come over to the United States.

An old boyfriend of Shira's was a producer on *Weeds.* Shira had met him on set, years ago when the show was new. She had a small role as a drug addict from Encino.

There is a rumor her ex is still in Los Angeles.

He might be in London.

Perhaps, Shira says, it would be nice to have a boyfriend she didn't have to pay to keep around. One successful in his own right and her own age.

Ayelet agrees with her. The cocaine has worn off and Ayelet is now so stoned her eyes have settled into permanent slits. When she wants to open her eyes, she raises her eyebrows instead.

Shira finds her ex-boyfriend's profile on Facebook and sends a friend request. On his profile are links to American articles praising his television show. Fans post their praise. Now and again, he responds. Shira scrolls through his page until finally she comes to the end and then she scrolls back up.

He is as handsome as when she knew him, twenty years ago.

But it *is* a professional shot.

If she squints and looks closely, she can see the signs of a receding hairline. The glimmer of a bald spot. And also his teeth really aren't that great. She is surprised he has not had them capped. She runs her tongue over her smooth, white-capped teeth.

Shira leaves Ayelet and the room. She walks out of the sliding glass doors to the patio and pool beyond. It is warm out, with that ever-present Los Angeles chill in the air. The sun is different in LA than it is in Jerusalem. It is more golden and more optimistic. Her credit card no longer works. She calls the bank in Israel using a calling card but the banks are closed. It is a holiday. They'll open again on Sunday. Where has her money gone? Has Asaf emptied that account? He does have her bank card. She'll have to move money from one investment to another. Certainly by tomorrow her check from her last acting gig will clear and the account will be replenished.

She thinks about visiting Marc and his family. She could take an Uber to Santa Monica. He could lend her money.

But she can't face her brother or Carolyn or their three perfect children. She misses Joseph. She promises to herself she will be extra kind to him when she gets back. She will be more patient with him. She is a good mom, she tells herself. When she gets home she will be even better.

On his third day alone, Joseph comes home from school after soccer practice. Mattan comes home with him. First, they create an elaborate video using the last four Lego sets his mother bought him: one from Tel Aviv, one from New York, one from Amsterdam, and one from the Malcha Mall in Jerusalem. Unfortunately, they are all different sets. It's not easy coming up with a scenario, but Joseph and Mattan manage. Better to be like his cousin Izaac, in America, who has four or five sets from each series and an entire room in the basement devoted to Lego setups. They use the program his father gave him to make an animated movie with his Legos. When they're finished they post the results to their YouTube channel. Joseph sends emails with a link to the YouTube video to everyone he knows. He sends a long email to his mother. Is there a chance you could come home earlier? he asks. Please? I have a game tomorrow. It is a big game, Ima, can you maybe come?

At dinnertime, Mattan goes home.

Joseph picks up the phone to call the restaurant. There is a knock at the door. He sets the phone down.

It must be his savta or saba or maybe his uncle Guy Gever, who is setting up some kind of art show nearby. He stepped on the balata some time ago and started to play with sticks and bushes and called it art. Everyone knows the legend of the balata, the crack in the pavement somewhere in the kibbutz. If

you step on the balata, you go mad. Joseph is very careful not
to step on cracks in the kibbutz.

Or maybe his father has remembered this was the week Joseph
was supposed to stay with him.

It could be Mohammed who has promised he'll come and
teach him poker one day.

Or perhaps Mattan has forgotten something?

Joseph knows one thing: Unless he knows who is behind it,
he mustn't open the door. That is the rule.

Joseph quietly pulls up a chair. He peers through the peephole
but sees no one. He hears a scrape at the door. A slight thud.
A shuffle. A voice.

Joseph. Joseph, are you there?

It's a man's voice and Joseph doesn't recognize it.

Joseph tiptoes to his bedroom and climbs the ladder to the
top bunk. He pulls the covers over his head. He thinks of
those children in the Shoah hiding in cellars and haystacks.
The stone walls of the apartment are too thick for him to
hear if the voice is still calling him. It is just seven o'clock,
and Joseph is hungry.

After a long while, he falls asleep.

When he wakes again it is very late. It is well past midnight.
Joseph is starving and there is nothing to eat. The brasserie is
closed. The most he can hope for is to walk over to the pizzeria
and get himself a cheese slice topped with boiled eggs—his
favorite. But he is afraid to leave the apartment.

Joseph feels sorry for himself. He begins to cry. Maybe he
will go to his father's apartment. He can take a taxi there.

Under his bed, Joseph spots a ten-shekel coin. He ties up his shoelaces and opens the front door.

There are emails, text messages, and finally phone conversations. Shira and her ex-boyfriend Michael arrange to meet.

Ma kara? What happened to you? Michael is saying to Shira. They sit in the Ivy. He had picked Shira up in a car so fancy, so small and sporty and with the most beautiful tan leather seats, that it made Shira's teeth ache with longing. He hadn't wanted to go to the Ivy but Shira had insisted. Come on, he says. The Ivy? Hadshote etmol. Old news. But Shira read about it in *Vogue* and she wants to see it in person.

What has happened to you? Michael continues. You are a little fat. It's not very attractive. But I like the bolt-ons. Shira looks perplexed. Michael cups his hands to his own fit chest. She notices that he has waxed or shaved his chest. No tufts of hair peeking up around his now smooth collarbone. They look *marvelous*, he says.

He is still good-looking. He is so good-looking.

Nu? he says. Did I hurt your feelings? You used to be so much fun. You used to laugh at everything I said. Remember the concerts? The ecstasy? The raves? He smirks and winks. The sex?

Bevadai! she says. She is trying to keep things light.

I read the blogs about Avi Strauss. Your son looks just like him.

He is not Avi's son.

At tzodeket. Right. Michael smiles, a little maliciously. Your son looks just like a Strauss. Do you remember I used to work for Avi Strauss? On my last show. When I was still acting and before he started that political show. You remember. I saw him around town, in Hollywood, before he died. I think he was writing scripts for porn films. Michael smirks again. When he smirks he looks like a ferret.

I remember everything, Shira says.

They leave the restaurant and wait for the valet to bring his car.

He tells her he wants to show her his place.

You'll like it, he says.

The apartment is an industrial loft in downtown Los Angeles. Michael pulls her through the living room to the bedroom. The floors are made of concrete.

He whispers, Maybe we can make a baby, huh? Would you like to make a baby with me?

It is a funny way to seduce. She's always wanted a second baby. Where is Joseph right now? She knows but doesn't want to know that Michael is lying. She'd like to believe he could fall in love with her. She closes her eyes and believes it.

He takes a long time, pounding away at her inefficiently. They finish. He picks up a small, white object. An electric cigarette. He puts it in his mouth and now, thinks Shira, he really looks like a faggot. Shira sits up and leans back on her elbows. The loft is spectacular. The windows are floor-to-ceiling tiny beveled glass. The light comes in and splashes color all over the gray rooms. Everything in the apartment is gray but the light. Shira pulls the blanket up over her shoulders and covers her breasts. There are no pictures on the walls.

She takes a drag off his electric cigarette.

He says, Why don't you stay here and let me help you get into shape? What are you living off there in haaretz? Burekasim and glidot? Too much hummus and pitot? I read about that thirty-year-old kid, Boulboulim, you are fucking in the gossip blogs. That situation is doing you no favors, I assure you. It only ages you by contrast. Come stay with me. It will be like a rehab. A spa. We'll get you into fighting shape again.

Fuck you, she says. I can't leave my son. You don't know anything about kids, she says.

Why not? I have a child.

Where?

In New York. I see her once a month.

Pfft.

All right then, Shiri. Tell me what it is you want?

What does Shira want? A meal, a man, a diversion, a mirror, some stroking. She'd like a large glass of red wine. She'd like a spliff. A real cigarette. She'd like more money. She'd like love. Someone her own age. To be young again. It doesn't do well to say what she wants.

I have everything I want, she says.

Streetlights through the jeweled glass of the loft's windows. Shira rummages through her bag and lights a cigarette. It is almost morning. She feels hungry and ancient. The salad from the Ivy had not filled her up. She longed for bread, for pitot and cheese and a glass or two of wine. But she is determined to go back home fitter and thinner than when she left. She sits up in bed and feels her breasts and her soft, fat stomach against the tops of her thighs. Michael is in AA and doesn't have any wine or marijuana or any food at all. There is a can of Diet Coke in the fridge and nothing more. She searches in vain through her purse for a Xanax. Michael orders in bagels and lox. Shira's hand snakes down to her belly. Ugh, she thinks. Bagels are the worst kind of carbs. But she is starving and wolfs down the bagel and reaches for a second. You need to stay here in Los Angeles, baby, he says. I can introduce you to my trainer. Maybe tomorrow we could do a SoulCycle class. Should I make a reservation? Shira shakes her head, no. I'm on vacation, she says. They have sex again.

She fakes all her orgasms.

In bed he's not as good as Asaf Boulboulim. Michael has already become too American, imagining he is the best lover in the world without doing a damned thing.

Still, she could live here. She could be happy here. She can feel what it would be like to live in that big empty apartment, so much bigger than her place in Jerusalem. She could have Joseph come on holidays. . . .

Can I make a phone call? she asks Michael. To Israel.

Sure, he says.

It's five o'clock in the afternoon in Jerusalem. Shira dials the number of her ex-boyfriend, Joseph's father.

Can I talk to Joseph please? she asks her ex-boyfriend's new wife.

He's not here, the new wife says coldly.

Are you sure?

Of course, she says. Our week is next week. I keep up with my children. Why? Where are you?

Her chest constricts and the salmon, cream cheese, and starch turn cold in her stomach. Never mind, she says.

Shira hangs up the phone.

She wails into her cupped hands, *Where is Joseph?*

Hello, Joseph.

Joseph cries out and tries to shut the door. A soldier jams his rifle between the door and the frame.

The phone is ringing.

Joseph stands stunned. He leans with all his weight against the door. He begins to scheme. He thinks he could slip past the soldier and grab his slice of pizza. He is still so very hungry. And maybe he will, yes, maybe now he will go to his father's house—in the Old City. He'll walk there if he has to. If this were Minecraft, he would create a portal. It would open up beneath his feet and deliver him to safety. To food, warmth, shelter.

Joseph, the soldier says on the other side of the door. I'm not going to hurt you. Don't you know me? I am your brother, Gabriel Strauss.

Chapter 5

LITTLE BLUE FLOWERS

CAROLYN WAS stoned, alone and stretched naked across the bed. Her eyes burned. She balanced her laptop on her belly and Googled "weed and skin damage."

Voices from downstairs floated through the floorboards. Carolyn's father had just arrived from Ohio. The children were protesting their baths and bed.

Marc opened the door of their bedroom and then quickly shut it behind him. Holy shit, it smells like Venice in here. Aren't you supposed to be finishing your marketing presentation? He opened the windows in the room. You didn't have all this pot when the police came, I hope.

No, Izaac's guitar teacher gave it to me when he heard what happened to us. Wasn't that nice of him?

Listen. You never told me you used to be a stripper. He reached for the jay and took a long drag.

Excuse me?

Your father told me just now downstairs.

Are the children asleep?

Marc shrugged. No.

Well, it's not true. I can't even think why my father would say such a thing, unless he was drunk?

That's a possibility. He did drink all of my Blue Moons. He asked me to make him a martini. He told me after you moved to New York, you were surrounded by trust-fund kids, and you felt you deserved their lifestyle. You asked your parents for money and when they said no, you became a stripper. I guess it's good we moved to LA, huh? You won't meet any of your old clients.

No.

No what?

I was never a stripper. Carolyn reached for the joint and flicked off the ash and brushed it off the coverlet on the bed. The truth is, I was a prostitute.

Very funny.

No, really.

This your father failed to mention to me.

That's because it didn't happen. I'm lying. She stretched out alongside him and held his hand a moment, massaging the web of skin between his forefinger and thumb. But it turns you on, doesn't it?

You'll have something to fall back on, if things get really bad. If I go to jail. Listen, have you called your old boss back? I thought he really liked you.

The next day, Marc took the boys to Hebrew school, and her father joined them.

Carolyn stayed home hidden in her bedroom and got high.

For the next hour she was lost. She searched her house as though she'd never lived there before. She opened drawers and poked through her father's things. She spaced out in the shower until the water ran cold, and then again standing in her closet with one leg in her jeans. Marc brought the kids home and she stole away upstairs again, locked the bedroom door, opened the windows, and took a lung-searing drag. She could hear her three boys shouting at one another downstairs—Don't *hit* me! He hit me!—and she decided to hide out until Marc screamed back at them, or one of them got hurt, listening for the inevitable tears. She put the joint into the drawer of the antique table that held the television and then sat cross-legged on the floor. She could almost see the ocean through the trees. It was early November. The window was cracked open and the sea air chilled her collarbones. Her husband walked into the room.

What are you doing? Marc asked her.

I'm meditating, she told him. He gave her a queer look.

So, is it your day off or what? We need to get lunch on the table before the boys' soccer practices. And *your* dad is downstairs and frankly, I'm tired of listening to him. I have enough on my mind. You can't fall apart every time your father comes to visit. And you can't fall apart on me when things are so difficult right now.

Right, she said. I know. I'm sorry. I'll be better.

When I was young, I thought I'd done everything right, the art director had told Carolyn, six months earlier on the day she'd quit her job. He'd once made short films that had won awards in film festivals. He'd published a small book of poems with a tiny San Francisco press. Now he provided a good living for his family. He helped with the kids. When they were small, he'd given his wife weekend mornings off to sleep. And she doesn't even work! he told Carolyn. They sat in his office, scattered with various industry awards. His elegant fingers drummed up and down the Formica desktop and Carolyn became transfixed by their rhythm. Tall and long-limbed, Christopher appeared a decade younger than his actual age. He wore thick black glasses and had blue, dogged eyes. He was the exact opposite physical type from her shorter, stockier, swarthier financier husband, who was right then texting her, demanding that she hurry up and get home before he *killed* someone. Marc was Mediterranean, hot-tempered and impatient. The desk clock read 7:00 p.m. She looked down at her phone. Six angry yellow faces marched across the screen.

Do you need to answer that? the art director asked. This is a long work day, I guess.

She shook her head. The dings and pings and, finally, ringing continued. Carolyn just wanted to sit and talk about art with the art director. Energy pulsed through her. She'd never felt better in her life.

Christopher lowered his head slightly and pushed her portfolio toward her. The folder stuffed with her drawings grazed her fingertips, almost like a caress. I love what you've shown me, he said.

Well. I worked hard, she said. Have to keep myself relevant.

Oh come on, really. You should see about getting a gallery opening.

Carolyn thought then about her coworkers, young kids newly minted from CalArts and UCLA. They lived night and day in the office and had time for their own art ambitions too. She thought about their Silver Lake houses, their rooms with no furniture and keg parties. Their downtown LA art gallery openings curated by kids born the year she graduated from high school. I'm too old for this, Carolyn said.

I don't think so, he said. He swiveled around and glanced at his computer screen.

You think you're too old for a comeback, she said. He had once been a rising star on the art scene.

I am.

Well, I'm much too old for a debut, then, don't you think? Too old to be an ingénue. After all, women age more quickly than men.

Not true. Men die younger.

I'm not talking about dying, I'm talking about aging. You and I are the same age, roughly, right?

Forties, more or less. Okay mid. Mid to late.

As a fortyish man you're young. As a fortyish woman I'm old. Think for a moment. You'll see I'm right.

I think you look great. A vacuum droned in the hallway outside his closed door. And—I think this is going to be a great campaign. She glanced down again at her phone and he said, You probably need to be going.

No, she said. My babysitter has left already. My husband is holding down the fort.

Really? he said. My wife would get quite shrill whenever I was late getting home. Especially when my kids were small. Carolyn had met his wife at the Christmas holiday party. She looked like she had been created with a scalpel.

They sat quietly and an intimate, awkward moment passed between them. Carolyn thought, if he wants to kiss me, I'll let him.

Carolyn. You know, I've always felt close to you, like I could really talk to you, really tell you what's on my mind.

Carolyn nodded. Her throat had gone very, very dry.

He continued: I don't even know how it happened! One minute she was making copies. It was late. No one else was in the office. I was grabbing my coat and the next thing I know I'm pressing her up against the machine and—

The intern. The one her best work friend called "tits on a stick."

She's a lovely girl, a really lovely girl. It's like, it's like she gets me, you know? I feel understood in a way I haven't felt in years. I mean, you know how marriage is after a while. The kids, the work, the constant arguing, negotiating for sex. I feel younger than I've ever felt!

The waistband of Carolyn's skirt tightened against her middle. Her carefully straightened hair was curling up at the fine sweat that had broken out at her temples.

It's not just an office fling. I really feel there's something more. The kids are all out of the house and . . . Sometimes I think my wife would just feel relief if I left her. Sometimes I get the feeling—

Yes, she said. I guess I do need to get going, as though he'd never spoken, as though he weren't in the middle of his sentence.

He had looked up at her then, surprised by her interruption. The air was thick with something she couldn't name, a possibility, or a chance to be illuminated. When I was young, I was a stripper and a call girl, she said.

He shuffled the papers on his desk, gathered up her drawings and handed them back to her. He was embarrassed, his face flushed red. He didn't meet her eyes. He mumbled something to Carolyn but she'd already stood up. She would never go back. That was six months ago.

She'd had enough.

After lunch, Carolyn went back upstairs and took a long shower. When she came downstairs, Marc was sitting with her father in the living room. She could see the pontificating look on her father's face; he was holding his breath, waiting for his daughter and her husband to say hello to each other so that he could finish whatever it was he'd been saying. Can I make you a drink, Dad?

I'll have an old-fashioned. Got any good whiskey? her father called out. He grabbed hold of her wrist as she swept through the room gathering toys and newspapers and soda cans. Her father smiled up at her, and then dropped her wrist and looked down at his lap. It's good to switch it up with alcohol. That's how you avoid becoming an alcoholic, he said.

Carolyn slipped down the hallway to the guest room en route to the kitchen. Her father's Dopp kit of toiletries sat open on the dresser. Rummaging through it, she pulled out two amber bottles: sleeping pills and an old painkiller prescription of her mother's. She hesitated a moment and then shoved several pills into the pocket of her pants. The source is limited, she thought to herself. He'll leave and take his pills with him. It's not like she could become addicted. She stood in the hallway between the guest room and the kitchen, listening to her father drone on and on. With a little Percocet, she could listen to her father all night. Marc's hostility settled over her in waves. He must be so pissed, she thought.

She took one of the painkillers and bit off a tiny sliver. Swallowing it dry. Empty bottles of beer sat on the kitchen counter and Carolyn rinsed them and threw them into the recycling bin. She took out two lowball glasses, the good whiskey, and the sugar bowl. She would add lots of sugar. Her father loved sugar. She pulled a wooden muddler out of a drawer and crushed two of the sleeping pills into the bottom of one of the glasses.

Hello, Mommy. It was her six-year-old, the baby, Nicholas. The other two were upstairs playing Minecraft or Skyping with their cousin Joseph. He stood holding onto the counter. She kissed the top of his head.

Hello, love. Did you stay with Grandpa today?

Yes, but we mostly watched television. The boy pointed to the glass. What's that? He started to reach for it but she swatted his hand away. Why are you crushing candy into that glass?

72

It most certainly is not candy.

Can you make me a snack?

You can watch an hour more of television and I'll bring it to you.

She poured a generous shot over the crushed tablets and a less generous shot into the second glass, added water and ice and heaping spoonfuls of sugar, and carried the two glasses into the living room.

Here, Dad, she said.

He took it from her midsentence without a pause. She handed the second glass to Marc, who glanced at her and raised his eyebrows. She squatted on the ottoman by the fire. Nicholas called for his snack. I'll get it, Marc said, and slipped away into the kitchen. Abba bah! he called out. Abba is coming.

When her father finished telling his story, he turned to Carolyn and said, I fixed a bottle opener for you, down in the basement. It's nailed to the wall next to the refrigerator where you guys keep all that Mexican pop. I also replaced those light bulbs in the basement bathroom. Trying to pay my rent for my time here. He coughed nervously and then fell into silence. Worried about you guys, you know. Hope it's not as bad as it sounds. Her father gestured to a framed poster on the wall. Is that a new print? he asked.

Yeah, from the Getty.

Who is it?

No one you'd know.

It's nice. That's an expensive frame. I guess Marc must have been doing well for himself. He drained his glass and rested it on his stomach. It's a shame neither of us had any real talent. His eyes closed heavily.

Her father listed over onto the arm of the couch. Dad?

She stood and took the glass from his hand.

He half opened his eyes and waved her away. Remember at the Art Institute? In Chicago? I think you were a teenager. Your sister was still alive. High school, maybe. Remember the painting we saw? All that grotesque flesh of old people and ordinary people? The wrinkles, the sagging skin, and I was proud not to look that way. I never thought I would. At your age you never think you'll get old. You never think you'll die. You think you'll be prepared when you finally do. You'll be done with being young, but you never are. You're never done being young. It's not that I want to be immortal. I just want to go back to that time before I knew I would die. You know?

Yes, Carolyn thought, closing her eyes.

Smaller Than Tears Are the Little Blue Flowers, she said. That was the title of the painting.

He snapped his fingers. That's it. Ivan Albright. Your mother thought it was hideous.

I thought it was beautiful.

His eyes widened. So did I. Isn't that wonderful? His eyes focused on hers. Something burned between them. So did I.

I miss Mom, Carolyn said. I wish she were here through all *this*.

Do you? he said. I wondered if you did.

He nodded and rested his head on the top of the couch, staring up at the ceiling with glazed eyes. After a few moments, his eyes closed and he began to snore.

Carolyn sat across from him and watched him a moment. His skin was still firm with a high color. He had a full head of reddish-blond hair, shot through with white around the temples. His shoulders were broad from daily swimming at the university pool back in Cleveland, where he still taught art history. He refused to retire. But her mother, who had aged so much faster than her father, was gone forever. And her sister, killed in a car accident ten years ago—also gone forever. Her father snored on like that. His hands, which he held stiffly in his lap, relaxed and fell to his sides. It was too warm in the living room. Carolyn lowered the downstairs thermostat and headed upstairs to the bedroom.

Marc was downstairs in his office. Even through the thick walls of their house she could hear him yelling at someone in Hebrew. Probably one of his employees, one of the few who'd stuck around. Or maybe one of the lawyers. She lit up a joint and sank into the down pillows of her bed. Tomorrow she'd try and get her old job back. If not, she'd go downtown and see if she could find a job. Maybe they could move back to New York and she could go back to marketing. It wasn't much money, but it would help. If things really went south, she'd be the breadwinner.

Chapter 6

THE FIRM

IN HIS Los Angeles asset management firm's office, Marc Solomon checks his email. Checks his stocks. Finds a song he likes on his playlist. His wife would laugh if she heard it. Why do all Israeli singers sound like Leonard Cohen? she would ask. Or Neil Diamond? Plaintive bleating.

He checks Facebook, which he has finally joined. His brother-in-law, Guy, looks to be doing well these days. He has a show in a gallery in Tiberias. His brother Dror still does not accept his friend request. His oldest brother, Ziv, is not on Facebook. He finds a friend request from Maya Frank. He accepts. They have several friends in common. She is married now five years. From the photos, she looks good. He'd heard from his mother of Maya's troubles: her failures in Amsterdam, the suicide attempts, the near drowning. She was once a real cusit. She was the only girl in the kibbutz who swallowed.

That's what he told his friends.

The myth was that every commando had a diamond under their zayin, between his balls, his baitsim. The trick was to keep fucking until someone found it. Now he loves his wife. He loves his three boys. He is not going to contact Maya Frank. After all her troubles, she is married now. In fact, she is married to one of his old friends, another commando, Levi Cohen. In fact, Cohen is now the commanding officer of their old unit.

But Maya is also rumored to be sleeping with Shai Skymatsky—another commando and Marc's best friend. If it's true—and nothing surprises him anymore—then he will have nothing to do with her.

But then, there is the message she sent him. How she'd had some bad times and how all was well now. She was trying to remember who she was when she was happiest and, as a matter of fact, she was last happiest when she was with him. She shouldn't have written that of course. Perhaps it was the wine that had gone to her head. She hoped he was well.

A cup of coffee next time he's in Jerusalem would hurt no one. Or where does she live now? Tel Aviv?

Marc's only real regret about leaving haaretz is that he misses the reserves and his buddies there. He misses the war games, the respect, *a world without women*. The soggy mess kits flooded with sea. Shai Skymatsky, who once held a wet schnitzel in his hands, wrung the seawater out into the sea, and devoured it in a single bite. Shai Skymatsky whose youngest brother, Tomer, now works in Marc's firm.

Marc Solomon loves his wife. He loves his children. He signs out of Facebook. Goes back to Ynet. Reads the news and gossip there.

The men in Marc's office throw down a few cognacs. They are a decade younger than Marc, most of them. Young, hungry men. They eye his assistant, Molly. They place their bets in an office pool. Marc hates the Lakers, though he respects Kobe Bryant. The Knicks are terrible. LeBron has left Miami and plays now for Cleveland. Marc is a lifelong fan of the Bulls. Tomer Skymatsky comes into his office. Nu? He asks. You betting? Marc shakes his head no. No thanks, man, Marc says. You know I don't gamble.

Every day in the financial markets is a gamble, Tomer Skymatsky says. He smiles his slanted smile. Tomer makes a lot of money for the company. He has a lot of Orthodox friends who invest money. They invest their donations in Marc's firm. Tomer is ambitious and wants to start a hedge fund. Hedge funds are where the money's at, Tomer says. Go big or go home. When Tomer goes to visit the religious, he wears religious garb: a kippa on his head and tzitzit dangling from his waist. Tomer knows how to charm.

Today is Friday and Tomer is dressed casually. More casually than anyone else in the office would dare. Marc needs to speak to him. Tomer wears jeans in the odd style of the Israeli youth. Skintight, but sagging at the crotch, halfway to his knees. Marc will have to talk to him about the dress code, even if it is casual Friday. This is a financial firm, not Shenkin, Marc will say. Not Burning Man.

Marc doesn't want to think about personnel problems or family problems. He goes back to his numbers. The numbers. Numbers are pure. Numbers are like diving in the navy. Watch the watch, watch the compass, watch the bubbles, watch the phosphorescence. Find the mark. Check the time. Count each kick of the leg. These things tell him the nature of reality but leave out this longing. This dissatisfaction with everyday life. Every day is a gamble indeed.

There is a knock on the door and a man enters. He's not been invited, or announced by Marc's secretary. The man is followed by another man and another. They are dressed in unfashionable denim and cheap leather shoes. These men fill his office. There are perhaps a dozen. A policeman enters last. LAPD. They speak English rapidly, too rapidly for Marc to catch what they are saying. The policeman is coming around Marc's desk and he is taking hold of both Marc's arms and pinning them behind him. The cuffs are cold around his wrists but the metal burns him and this is another thing Marc doesn't understand and cannot make sense of.

In the West Bank, they used plastic cuffs for arrests.

He sits at his desk with his hands pinned behind his back. A man who is a detective sits on his desk in front of him. The detective is telling him that his house is being searched at this moment. He asks Marc what the detectives in his house will find. Will the detectives find drugs in his house? Are there guns in the house? Most important, the detective asks about money. As in, Where is the safe, Mr. Solomon? Where is the safe hidden?

Can I speak to my wife? Marc asks.

In a minute, yes. We'll let you speak to your wife. As long as you cooperate.

What am I charged with?

You know what you are accused of.

Everyone in Marc's office is ordered to turn over their laptops, tablets, and cell phones. Every employee's bags are emptied. Computers are taken and passwords are written down. Finally, his secretary manages to secretly call his attorney, who hears the police questioning Marc Solomon. Within an hour his attorney is in the office demanding Marc be read his rights. He tells Marc not to say another word. The detectives tell him what he's accused of. A large betting pool run through his office. It might be international. Is it international? they ask Marc. The more you tell us now, they say, the better it will be for you. Spreadsheets on *his* server. Money is missing. *A large amount.* What's the password, Solomon? All the computers have been seized.

The detectives tell Marc that one of his employees, Tomer Skymatsky, has already explained everything to them.

But he was just here! Marc says. He is the brother of my best friend! Marc gets up to search for him. He was just here! You can ask him yourself.

Easy, guy, the cops say. They push him down in the chair. Nice office you got here, Solomon, they say. We were expecting something a little less sophisticated.

A detective hands Marc a cell phone. He can hear Carolyn's flat voice. Marc? she says. She doesn't sound desperate. Good, Carolyn, Marc thinks.

Marc says, It will be all right. Tell them everything. We've done nothing illegal and we have nothing to hide. It's a mistake, Marc says. A misunderstanding. The lawyers will handle everything.

Don't worry.

Chapter 7

Gabriel

I N SPITE of Gabriel's high SAT scores, he hadn't bothered to apply to any colleges. He'd been scouted by UCLA and Stanford for soccer scholarships, but for Gabriel Strauss college was to be deferred three years so he could enlist in the IDF, like his father would have wanted. Then, if he liked Israel and his Hebrew improved, he could attend university there.

The army had not been so bad and then suddenly, it was unbearable. It was hellishly hot in the green army cotton and the black boots that laced up to his calves. The gun was hellishly heavy. If he could have mustered up some kind of moral outrage against the IDF as so many of his Israeli friends back home in California had, it would have been all right. *We should just get the fuck out of the Middle East*, they'd said, passing the vape. *What right have we to be there?* they'd said. But he couldn't not go.

It was hot all the time. The sweat dripped down his forehead. His forehead had broken out in vicious acne. He hated to wake up early. He was spoiled. All right, he admitted it: He was far more spoiled than the young Israeli men around him. They all seemed grown-up compared to him. He was soft, just as his brothers had said, but how was that his fault exactly? His father had brought them to California, and then he'd died.

Then the showers. Always the best part of the day. He'd stood there as long as he could get away with. The guys around him, all mostly too tired even to speak. He couldn't say he was even thinking of anything at the time. Maybe he'd thought of Sophia Allen, Sophia Allen and her sister, or a female officer he'd developed a crush on. He really couldn't say. But there he'd stood. His cock rose. *He got a fucking erection in the fucking showers in the fucking barracks of the IDF.* You going to bugger us in the shower? Eli Rabin had called out. Eli Rabin who reminded Gabriel of the oldest and most sadistic of his three brothers.

Gabriel had been mortified. Perhaps he should have covered himself and run off somewhere, instead of what he'd done, which was to stand there bathed in shame until the hot water turned cold and everyone had finished and left.

Never too popular with the other young soldiers, who were *real* Israelis, Gabriel was teased mercilessly.

One night, a few weeks after the shower incident, just before weekend leave, the commanding officer sent word that Gabriel was to meet him in his office.

The office ceiling was low. Fluorescent tubes hung over them. They buzzed and flickered. It was humid. The concrete walls sweated the salty moisture of the sea. The desk was metal and the commanding officer sat behind it, leaning back in his chair, with his boots on the desk. His hands clasped the back of his head in a studied, casual alpha pose. He fired off some words in rapid Hebrew but Gabriel was nervous and didn't immediately understand. Ma?

Is this how you speak to your commanding officer?

Lo, Ha'mefaked!

Listen, Strauss. I'm going to tell you a funny story since I know who your father was. There was once a Moroccan boy, you know, Sephardi, who came home from school. He said, Ima, I knew the answers to fifteen math questions. The other kids knew only ten. Is this because I'm smarter than them? The mother said, No, that's not the reason. The next day the boy came home from school. Ima, today I knew twenty vocabulary words and the other kids knew only fifteen. Is it because I'm smarter than them? No, his mother said. That's not the reason. The next day the boy came home from school. Ima, my zayin—you know that word, yes? Penis!—is twice as big as the other boys'. What is the reason for this? She said, it is because you are twelve and the other boys are eight.

Gabriel's throat dried and he coughed.

What? the mefaked said. You are Ashkenazi, yes, Strauss? Are you offended? People don't joke around in America? Where is your mother from?

My mother is from Fez, sir. But— It's very funny, sir, Gabriel said.

Do you know why I have called you here tonight?

Lo, Ha'mefaked!

That's right, you don't know. I've heard about your shower incident. The mefaked smiled a small, greedy smile. Nu! You will have your weekend leave and on Sunday morning, you will report to duty first thing. You have an interesting new assignment that will suit you very well. You will go to Yitzhar to the settlements. Of course, you will have to protect yourself from them as well. They are no less than domestic terrorists. Many of them are Americans like you. Last week they slashed the tires of our jeep. The children throw stones at the soldiers. The *Jewish* children. But as an American, I think this assignment is very suitable. Yes, he said, tapping his fingers together in front of his temples. This is a suitable assignment for you.

The mefaked leaned back just a little more in the chair, as if to stretch his small barrel-like chest, and then, before Gabriel's eyes, the mefaked toppled backward.

He cried out like an animal. Gabriel stood and staggered a few steps toward the door. The mefaked shouted to him in English, Come here, you motherfucker!

And Gabriel was running, shouting, *Lo, Ha'mefaked! I'm sorry! Slicha!* behind him as he ran to his barracks and to his bed.

He lay awake all night wondering what would happen, wondering if he would be punished. He was supposed to go on weekend leave to his aunt's house in Yemin Moshe for Shabbat. But they were religious and that meant twenty-four hours with no television, computers, or cell phones. They were Ashkenazi which meant the food would be bad. He missed his mother's cooking. The Moroccan fish and cholent cooking all night in the oven for Shabbat. Ima, he thought, sadly.

The following day he was free on leave. He agonized a moment. If he stayed on base, he could travel into the city and see a movie, perhaps walk around the nearby kanyon, the mall, to try and meet a girl or buy a T-shirt. He could perhaps go see the boy and his mother. He could not bear to go to his aunt's house. Almost like an army base in its austerity. He left his aunt a message. Something came up, he told the voice mail, relieved he didn't have to talk to her. He had to stay on base for the weekend.

He took a bus to the Jerusalem mall in the neighborhood of Malha.

It was Thursday night, the start of the weekend, and the streets were filled with kids, families, and soldiers. Everyone in everyone's face. Jews and Arabs. He ate a falafel sandwich and walked an hour until he'd reached the Moshava Germanit neighborhood, where he found Shira and Joseph's apartment building.

He'd known where she lived, his father's ex-girlfriend Shira. The one Gabriel's father had right before he'd moved the family to Los Angeles so he could sit in a studio office and write his screenplays. Gabriel had found her address, on a package she'd sent to his office full of the Turkish coffee he loved so much. On a couple of Gabriel's weekend leaves, he'd sat on a bench outside her apartment sipping espressos he'd bought from a kiosk. It was a pleasant neighborhood. Israeli girls raced by on Rollerblades with their tan skin and sharp elbows. There were dogs and children everywhere. People were more relaxed here than in America. It was difficult to explain. It was cool and restful beneath the trees on the fashionable streets of Jerusalem.

He knew what they both looked like, Shira Solomon and her son, Joseph. The two of them had recently been in the newspaper for participating in various protests. The boy was pictured holding up signs at rallies. Gabriel had found another photo of the two of them participating in a Tel Aviv sit-in protesting Palestinian prisoners. The boy looked so much like his mother it was hard to know who his father might be.

Making his way through the streets, Gabriel decided he was not going back to the army. He was not going to continue to protect settlements and live in misery. No. He was going back to Los Angeles. His brothers, his mother, and his commanders, the other soldiers and even his dead father, Baruch Hashem, could go fuck themselves.

Chapter 8

GAN EDEN

L ONG AGO when the kibbutzim were thriving, children could choose either sandals or tennis shoes twice yearly. Along with their new shoes, they could choose between one new pair of sweatpants *or* jeans made in a nearby kibbutz that were ill-fitting and stiff. Most chose sweatpants. The children lived in a children's house, separated from their parents from the age of three months. The house was called Gan Eden, the Garden of Eden.

On Friday, just before Shabbat began, each child in Gan Eden received a small bar of Elite chocolate. Marc was careful to hide his under his cot where he kept his tachtonim and socks. If another child found it, they would eat it. A terrible betrayal. The metapelet had no sympathy for him or anyone.

In the children's house, he was a weeper. In every children's house there was a child who cried all night, and for two years, Marc was that child. He missed his mother, and he knew his mother missed him. But Shira, who was one year older, liked the metapelet better than their mother, or pretended to, and she made every effort to let her mother know it. Later Shira would realize the metapelet didn't care about anyone at all, except maybe her husband, Omri, the moreh who taught English and was the most handsome man in the kibbutz. Marc would let no one comfort him and the metapelet spent the evenings next door in the lul with her hand rolled cigarettes, ignoring the intercom. Mornings the metapelet was rank with chicken shit. Or so the children said. The older children joked that she must have been fucking the head of the lul—her husband's best friend—right on top of the chicken feed, that she used the plumpest chicken to prop up her hips while they did it.

Marc Solomon was popular and well-liked. Eventually, he learned to repress his tears when insulted or afraid at night. He was good at sports, reasonably okay in class work. Class work was never as important to a kibbutznik as the ability to work hard.

The kibbutz was small. There was nothing to do for entertainment but talk about one another and Shira was frequently talked about. From Marc's earliest memories Shira either sang too loudly, talked too loudly, or shouted. It seemed that there was nothing she wouldn't do for attention. By the time she was twelve years old, she was already wearing her shirts hanging off her narrow shoulders, and stealing her mother's lipstick. She had long, expressive legs. She was going to be a famous dancer when she grew up. Or an actor. Or a rock star. Or a painter. She was talented enough to do all those things. She hung around older boys and smoked cigarettes. She tore up the kibbutz jeans and had Vivienne alter them so they were tight around her skinny legs. Marc found her excruciating to look at—even more terrible was that he *wanted* to look at her.

In the kibbutz to be self-effacing was regarded highly. It was even better to be invisible if you could manage it. Shira could not manage it. When she was not calling attention to herself, she was breaking objects. She broke dozens of cups in the dining room, and plates seemed to rain down at her feet. Mazel tov! the kibbutz would call out, Mazel tov! as another glass shattered on the white-tiled floor of the dining room.

Her presence in the kibbutz was always felt.

Marc, on the other hand, was capable of doing only what he was told to do. He was the good boy. The best. He did everything right, everything with care. He put his head down and tried not to notice Shira. He tried not to notice the diary in her bag on their annual Pesach trip to the Red Sea. He wasn't going to read it, he wasn't going to. He was a good boy.

Back then, Marc wore his hair long and bushy. Shira took an iron to her black, curly hair and wore it straight, like Cher.

Their father, Yakov, liked to say Shira's mouth ran in front of her legs. But her mouth and her legs were only the half of it. There was also her tachat and tzitzim, her tits and ass. Once Shira hit puberty, these were always where they were not supposed to be.

After her bat mitzvah, Shira graduated from the children's house to the apartments. She was no longer obligated to spend the daily three hours with her parents, and so she didn't. She never saw them at all. Unless Yakov had come home from a trip abroad, bearing gifts of Levi's and Lacoste shirts.

She received her first kibbutz job and went to work with the younger children at the ganon, the preschool. They would cry for their mothers at nap time. Shira would soothe them and sometimes sing to them, their soulful, sad eyes gazing back at her in mute misery. When she left for her own apartment at night, they clung to her. She would bring them glasses of cold fresh milk and smooth their foreheads. But sometimes she would get angry at them. Buck up, she'd whisper.

Many children chose to go to school barefoot eight months out of the year. School was not required, after a certain age, but merely a suggestion on the kibbutz. They were free to leave school if they liked, and work. Kibbutzniks were born to work hard. They would grow up to be the WASPs of Israel: Wellborn, Ashkenazi, Special Forces, Paratroopers. The children worked in the fields for one month of every summer. They helped with harvesting the apples, dates, and pomegranates. They spent their lives outside. Their children's books were translated Russian picture books from the thirties that showed healthy, strong blond children milking cows, collecting chicken eggs, shucking corn, hauling bales of hay. The kibbutzniks were the new Jews placed in the north and around the perimeters as a buffer between Syria and Lebanon and the rest of Israel, and they belonged to no God, but only the collective and the land that was historically theirs.

Later, Omri was Shira's favorite teacher. She fell in love with him when he cast her in a school production of the English play *Saint Joan* by George Bernard Shaw. Omri's hair stuck out

like steel wool around his narrow face. His chin ended in a
black arrowhead of a beard. His eyes were blue and he moved
like a big cat. Like his wife, the metapelet, he seemed not to
care about anyone or anything. He liked to hang out in the
cowshed, where he would smoke his hash pipe each morning
and the cows came wading through the shit and mud to greet
him. The only tenderness he displayed was for the baby calves
in their cages, crying for their mothers. He would sit on the
cement floor of the cowshed and bottle-feed them.

Marc could see Shira liked the moreh, the teacher. Shira who
could never do the normal thing and like a boy from her class,
or maybe two classes above. They said she lost her virginity to
Omri behind the lul. Marc's friend Baruch said they had done
it in a pile of chicken shit. But probably only because Baruch
was jealous. He'd always had a crush on Marc's sister.

His sister was a sharmuta. Their father, Yakov, heard everything. Their mother, Vivienne, was scandalized. She cried every
Tuesday night when Marc came to her house to eat lecho, the
Moroccan matbucho tomato salad, and watch *Little House on
the Prairie.*

They said the metapelet didn't care that her husband was
cavorting around the kibbutz with Shira. But when Omri and
Shira ran off to Tel Aviv for three days when Shira was only
fifteen years old, the metapelet threw herself off the water
tower. Some said she was high on mushrooms and thought she
could fly. She survived and was taken to the hospital in Sfat
and stayed there three weeks. The children in the children's
house were left alone for three nights before anyone noticed

that the metapelet needed to be replaced and that Shira was not coming to work. Yakov had Omri fired from his teaching job. He slunk around the kibbutz for years in disgrace. After the metapelet was released from the hospital she went back to New York, where it was said her father owned a department store on Fifth Avenue.

Marc went into the army and for years nearly forgot his sister existed. She was a shadowy thing, a source of gossip, finally.

Chapter 9

Shira and Marc in LA

S HE SAID to him, I've kind of run out of money. My money didn't come in from my last television job and something is wrong with my bank account. For some reason my investment account has not transferred into my bank account and I have no access until Monday. When I get back home the day after tomorrow I'll have to move some money around.

Shira was miserable. To ask for money from anyone made her sick to her stomach. But she needed just a little to tide her over a couple more days.

Marc was preoccupied. He fiddled with his phone and watched the young girls in their short dresses ordering complicated coffees. The café in the Standard was loud, the crowd around the register was growing, and everyone was so young and beautiful and à la mode. It could break your heart.

Marc had no time for her, Shira could see that. He stretched his leg under the table to get his wallet from his back pocket and accidentally kicked Shira in the shin. Shira winced but didn't say anything. There would be a bruise. Marc pulled out his billfold, giving her an apologetic look. He raised his eyebrows and pointed at the phone that vibrated audibly and often. What could he do? Marc Solomon was a very busy man. Today he looked especially preoccupied, even tortured. She tried to appear sympathetic. His hand was hovering over the bills. So many of them! The hundreds on top, of course. He counted the notes under his breath and Shira looked away. She would count them back in the room.

He covered the phone with his hand. Use it wisely, he said.

That was a dig. Shira wondered if Marc had heard about Asaf. But Shira could feel joy rising in her chest. She'd buy something grand for Joseph. Maybe an iPod or the pair of American sneakers he'd asked for. She felt the muscle of her heart spasming. Joseph. Yakov had found him finally when the credit card company called him about the airplane ticket charge that boy of Avi Strauss had made. He was safely at his furious father's apartment and Shira, humiliated and upset, could not wait to fly home.

You talk to Ima lately? Shira said, when Marc had finally set the phone down on the table.

Yes, he said. I speak to her every day.

You have always been such a mama's boy, Shira smiled. Ima's favorite.

I don't see Ima, Marc said. I am not *there*. And I am hardly a mama's boy. She could see he was getting angry.

Shira said, No, ach sheli, my brother. I'm sorry. I'm only jealous because after Ziv came out and moved to Singapore, you were Ima and Abba's favorite.

Have you heard from Ziv? Marc asked. I keep telling him to come to LA.

No, Shira said. Not in a while. Thank you so much for the money. She was ready to go.

Come on, now, Marc said. I wasn't the favorite! Hardly. And I was once so envious of you. You were older, Marc said. You know, you remind me a little of my wife.

Carolyn! No. I am nothing like Carolyn.

You are. You and she are impetuous and reckless.

Shira sat mulling this over. Of course, she was insulted. It is always this way when a man gives you things, she mused. He gives and in exchange you bow your head and accept his insults. Only prostitutes ever really get paid. But now Shira was angry.

Your children are spoiled, Marc. Your *wife* spoils them. Your oldest child has already had his bar mitzvah but has never even crossed a street on his own.

I know, Marc said. You are right. He shrugged and put his hands up. But what can I do? In America things are like this.

Yes, she said. America is more dangerous.

Maybe. I don't know. I don't think so. There are no natural enemies here, for instance. It is not as though we will go to war with Canada. No one worries about bombs here. Do you remember, Shiri, how we used to pray a bomb would wipe out the road to the school?

Or wipe out the school altogether, Shira said.

Marc signaled to the waitress again for the check. Shira thought of Joseph, safe, thank God. She said, In America children shoot up schools.

Yes, Marc said. This is true. The last one happened just twenty minutes from our old house in Connecticut. An elementary school too.

You should come back to Israel, Marc. Yakov and Vivienne miss you and they are getting old. And Joseph could use an uncle.

He has Dror, Marc said. He has Ziv.

No one has Ziv, Shira said. He won't come back until Yakov invites him. Shira picked up a spoon and stirred her coffee. Joseph could use an uncle, Shira said again.

Marc shook his head. Carolyn would never go there, he said. She would be miserable.

Shira laughed. Yes, she never looks too happy when she is there.

It's hard for her. The first night we stayed in the kibbutz, when she was pregnant with Izaac, I took her to a barbecue with the guys.

That doesn't sound very wise, Marc.

No, it wasn't very wise. There was all this delicious food spread out and all the guys were drinking a bottle of whiskey, just passing it between us. No glass. Baruch grabbed a handful of chicken wings and shoved them in his mouth. He spit the bones out into the corner of the barn. And then the wind kicked up and the smell of the lul filled the barn. Six cubic tons of chicken shit. She threw up all night long.

Horrible! Shira said. Those horrible, stupid chickens and the smell. Shira made a face.

No, Marc said. It's the best smell in the world. Give me early morning in the lul any day of the week and I'll take it. I look forward to getting back there.

Yes, Shira said, her face twitched. I'm sure Abba and Ima can't wait for you to come.

Marc looked pained. Shira, he said. It wouldn't hurt you to be nicer to Ima.

Shira stood up. Once, when they were small, she'd *owned* her brother. She glared down at him. Fuck you, little brother. Fuck you and fuck your American wife. Come back to Israel and see how perfect your parents are. Try and be the *daughter* of Vivienne and Yakov Solomon and see how great it is.

Shiri, please.

Everyone was staring and pretending not to. Shira glided out the door. Chin at an angle, shoulders squared. Her hand on the bulge of one-hundred-dollar bills in her front pocket.

Marc exhaled. His sister had always been like this. No one knew if she was born this way, or if she was molded by forces no one could foresee or control.

When things went bad in business, he assumed it was bad luck, and when his numbers looked good, he understood it was due to his intelligence and cunning.

He would get Shira her money back.

Marc thought about luck a lot these days. He thought of his company now—almost two hundred and fifty million under management—and felt a glow of pride, and then the stab of fear. No charges had been filed against him yet and every day, lawyers fought to get his money back. Every day, the prosecutors threatened to haul him in front of a grand jury. But one day he'd be dead and none of it—siblings, money, wife, children—none of it would matter. Marc would have to leave everything behind. It was unfair, wasn't it, that one day everything he'd ever done would mean nothing?

Chapter 10

THE PRETTY PAST

B ORIS WAS her manager. He told Carolyn she'd make five to six hundred dollars a night *easy*.

Boris gave her a new name: Susannah. "Sexy Susannah" was how the escort service billed her. She had her own ad with a photo of her legs half-obscured by a bit of fake fur tossed across her lap. Not *her* legs, actually, but a stock photo.

He said, You got a nice clean look. You'll make a lot of pesos.

In the beginning Carolyn stayed away from the cocaine Boris offered her—I can get you product, discounted—but she couldn't resist the Ativan. *Attagirl!* Boris called it. On her first night, he gave her an envelope with several inside. They give Ativan to people right before they go in for surgery, Boris had told her. It's addictive. Remember, he said, You only lose your virginity once. After that, you're a pro. He also warned her that after the first few times she'd feel high, and then she'd get depressed. But, it will all get better on payday.

Carolyn thought with the extra money and time during the day, she'd be able to work on her art.

Carolyn took a cab to the Midtown Marriott next to Grand Central. In the cab, she put her face on and pulled her fuck-me pumps from a large fake Prada bag she'd bought on Canal. She threw her flats into her bag. She'd wear them home. The pumps were impossible to walk in everywhere except the lobby of the Marriott, where the thick carpet absorbed them.

She had a tip for the doorman, who always looked lascivious, and a tip for the desk clerk, who was apparently embarrassed. She had the same room on the seventeenth floor six nights in a row and a pager. The pager had belonged to another girl before her and on the back had a glittery Hello Kitty sticker with the words FUCK ME embossed in red across its face. Hello Kitty had big fake-looking tits.

In her big fake Prada bag she carried makeup, hair spray, a skinny comb, a credit card machine, and condoms. She'd been instructed by Boris not to, in fact, use the special lipstick the makeup artist he'd hired told her to use. He explained, no man wants blood-red anything on his dick. She was instructed never to wear perfume. They've got wives to go home to.

Sometimes, just for fun, at home in her apartment, she put the special lipstick on her nipples.

The beeper beeped and someone would knock on the door. She would bring him in by the hand and sit him on the bed. She would shimmy around the room in her lace Agent Provocateur underwear doing a small striptease to the waist. The guy would lie down, his pants in a bunch around his knees. Big, small, red, brown, cut and uncut. Long and thin. Fat and short. Fat and long. Short and thin. The men waved them around with earnestness and confidence and hopelessness. It was ridiculous but Carolyn loved it. She loved them. She sat down beside them on the bed and for a little more money they could choose whether or not to fondle her tits. With her hand on their dicks, they came in two minutes easily. She learned some tricks. Astroglide. There was no actual vaginal or anal penetration. There was the occasional blow job, but it was expensive. She watched the digital clock next to the bed as she jerked them off. She rooted for them. Come on. Go three minutes. Come on. But they never did. She had an excellent hand-job technique, developed during her virginal high school years. Sometimes they liked music and she let them pick out the radio station.

One guy, barely out of high school, had completely white pubic hair. I can't dye it, he told her apologetically, or I'll get a rash. Another guy was desperately ashamed to have only one testicle. What is it with men and their testicles, she thought but didn't say. Who cares? Almost all were married. None of them thought what they were doing was cheating because there was no penetration.

Sometimes Carolyn longed to fuck them. It would have been, frankly, easier, faster and less effort somehow.

She didn't care, she didn't care. Let them wave their ugly dicks in the air. For her effort she got ninety dollars a session. She had five or six sessions a night.

In the beginning it wasn't boring. It was exciting and dirty and sometimes, after they'd all left and her shift was over, she'd turn over on her stomach and masturbate on the bed with a tiny vibrator Boris had given her. Let the steam out, he'd told her. She liked to imagine the best-looking guy from the evening pinning her to the bed and fucking her hard and brutally. She liked to imagine the ugliest guy tugging her hair and wrapping his fingers around her neck. One or two she imagined making love to her. Touching her tenderly and whispering, I love you. Maybe they would pick her up and take her home with them. This isn't the life for you, they'd say, and pay off her student loans. She would come with a mouthful of Marriott pillowcase and the taste of bleach between her teeth.

It took three or four months before she began to fall in love with them. The first was Alan, a Jewish lawyer with insane pecs and skinny legs he was self-conscious of. He showed her pictures of his kids in his well-worn wallet. Then it was Vinny, who gave her two hundred dollars extra for a blow job. Yer a good girl at heart, he liked to say, just before he came. He liked to tell her she was the classiest girl in the world. *I could take you anywhere, anywhere. Any club.* It was temporary. They were temporary. They came and went and then eventually they never came back. Boris told Carolyn not to take it personally. If they wanted one girl all the time they'd save their money, stay home and fuck their wives.

Boris started coming around after her shift. They'd go down to the lobby bar and have a drink: a glass of whiskey for Boris and a Long Island iced tea for Carolyn. Carolyn, Boris had said. What are we going to do with Carolyn? We got big plans for you. He said it with something that felt to Carolyn like sympathy. She started to look at Boris differently.

No doubt it was what he said to all the girls. Something you say to a girl whose premium hand jobs provide your living. Of course he thought she was pretty. He wanted to make money off of her. He'd approached her at that early spring street fair on Astor Place for just that purpose.

Her roommate Whitney said, Jesus, Carolyn. What the fuck is wrong with you?

After a while, after the men had all gone, and the last customer had left his used washcloth on the industrial carpet of the Marriott, it became so lonely. She'd light up a joint, masturbate, and watch television. Sometimes she'd pull out her sketchpad, but mostly she was uninspired. A lot of times she stayed the night there alone. The room cost her about twenty-five percent of her wages, but why not? Boris had offered to get her another girl to take the late night-early morning shift and split the cost of the hotel but Carolyn put him off. She thought about giving up her apartment with Whitney. She felt that Whitney was judging her. Maybe Whitney was jealous of all the money she was making now. Whitney had always had a lot more money than Carolyn. Whitney had a trust fund and a corporate lawyer boyfriend who was going to ask Whitney to marry him.

It took some time for Carolyn to realize that she was disappearing into all those hand jobs. Had she ever existed in the first place? It had only been six months since she'd quit her temp job. Six months since Boris had recruited her on a low day at the street fair. He'd bought the silk scarf she'd been eyeing with the impossible-to-comprehend price tag of fifty dollars. He'd asked if she was used to guys spending money on her. He told her she was worth much more than a lousy temp job. She had so much potential. Carolyn had wondered if he wasn't some kind of movie scout or modeling agent.

It seemed she'd never really been there in the Marriott, in her heels and discounted undergarments, smiling at her sheepish, silly patrons. She had floated above it all, disassociated, a voyeur of her own theatrics. A coping method she'd perfected long ago. Maybe it was all the Ativan she'd taken, the joints she'd smoked, the guys she'd jerked off. The hands on her tits. Their eyes suddenly blind and unseeing as they pulled up their pants, and sometimes left a tip on the dresser.

Maybe the high heels she wore had ruptured a vital, invisible artery to her heart. Or maybe the heart had never been there in the first place.

She spent more and more time with Boris. Boris with his gargantuan coke addiction. He swore at cabbies, was xenophobic—despite being an immigrant himself—and muttered racial epithets only just barely under his breath. Sometimes, to Carolyn's horror, he shouted at them. He'd started taking her out at midnight when she left the hotel, picking her up in a cab. He took her to good restaurants on her nights off. She began to put on weight. He'd stopped scheduling anyone the last hour of her shift so they could order bad room-service club sandwiches and maybe have a glass of vodka on the rocks from the minibar. He let her keep a larger and larger percentage of her wages.

He made love to her and Carolyn had never enjoyed making love—until Boris. She had generally always liked it quick and dirty. Come on my face and pull my hair. But Boris wasn't that kind of guy. He was the first guy to make her come by going down on her. He pressed the palms of his hands against her thighs, his fingers reaching up to the skin of her belly. He only brushed her with the back of his hand, as though he, and only he, knew that was the thing that drove her crazy. He was grossly unattractive. Bald with thin hairs that crept across his speckled skull like spiders' legs. Potbellied and so bowlegged he rocked from side to side down the carpeted hallway to the elevator. He was a full head shorter than her, but he had a huge cock. Most of the time, because of the Viagra-vodka-coke cocktail, he didn't come. But he knew what he was doing. It was all about Carolyn.

It had never been all about Carolyn.

First she'd fallen in love with the men, now she'd fallen in love with her pimp.

Are you fucking stupid? Whitney asked. Women like Whitney always struck gold. Her boyfriend had paid off her student debts, her credit cards, *and* gave her one thousand dollars a month spending money—and never saw hookers. No, never saw hookers, according to Whitney. Carolyn didn't say a word. Why, Carolyn wondered, wouldn't *any* guy rather see a hooker? Relationships were a misery. Whitney said—and she was right— You're not supposed to fall in love with your pimp. Even *I* know that. You should crawl right back to Cleveland.

Sure, she could. Carolyn had ten thousand dollars saved up in the six months she'd been working. It was stuffed in a safe-deposit box at the Chase branch on Park Avenue. The same bank that laughed at her just one year ago, chuckling away as they collected her overdraft and insufficient funds fees. She could do whatever the fuck she wanted.

Only later did she realize she'd never get what she really wanted.

Chapter 11

THE RESERVES

SHAI SKYMATSKY'S thighs stick to the vinyl seats of the little Toyota. He throws the car into reverse and heads down the beach road. He is still in his underwear. He is two hours late for the drill. The largest reserves drill the army has ever executed.

Every gear locks into place. The engine fires.

The sea crashes beside him. He cuts the lights.

A bottle of Sprite rolls on the floor. He picks it up, opens it, downs it, and tosses the bottle onto the seat. Tonight the entire military fleet will mobilize. The men will storm the beach north of Yaffo like four hundred horsemen of the apocalypse.

He loves his guys so much he sleeps with their wives.

Back on Avenue Viron, the woman who sleeps in his bed is small but bossy. She is in love with Shai Skymatsky. Maya belongs to the officer in charge of tonight's exercise, who is also his best friend. Her thighs gripped him tight. Don't leave, she said.

He fucks with the lights off.

That's what they say about Shai Skymatsky.

The surf crashes on the beach before him. The sand is littered with cigarettes. The ships bulk along the horizon. They are two miles out but he can make it. He can make it. He's not that late. He can make it.

He can't make it.

Skymatsky reaches into the back of his car for the empty soda bottle. He pulls out a flashlight and knife. He cuts the plastic bottle in half and fits it over the flashlight and runs to the edge of the beach, flashing the green light again and again. He waves his T-shirt over his head. The cold creeps into the fabric of his underwear and through the hair on his back and chest. The night has settled into the sea.

He jumps up and down, flashing his green Sprite light. What is he now?

A tiny bit of phosphorus.

An insect.

At sea, men slip from the ships into the velvet water. Others stand on the decks in slick black frog suits. They sit in the cockpits of Neshers. Some blink through binoculars. Some talk into radios. The air is biting cold but no one feels it. They are one long artery of adrenaline.

Something on shore, says an officer.

Never mind, says the officer in charge.

No, I'm seeing something. I see something right on the beach.

Never mind, says the officer in charge. Let's begin.

I don't think that would be prudent, sir.

Never mind, says the officer in charge.

Take a look, sir.

The officer in charge grabs the other officer's binoculars. Men in freezing water. Men piss their suits for warmth. Men in minisubmarines, submersibles, men in Zodiacs, waiting.

God help us. Something is on the beach, says the officer in charge. I see a green light.

Is it supposed to signify the enemy? the officer asks the officer in charge. Have the perimeters of the operation changed?

This was not the original plan, says the officer in charge.

Should we shoot it? Should I fire a short-range missile? Should I radio the snipers?

The officer in charge picks at his face with delicate fingers. That is not the plan, he says again.

Is it a drone? asks the officer. Is it a drone? Should we shoot it?

The officer in charge shrugs. He turns his pocked face to the sky and locates the constellations. There is no moon. The stars fire on all cylinders.

The officer stands beside the officer in charge. He adjusts himself. The tiny pin of green light dances on shore.

Operation will be moved. Two miles south.

Men are hauled up. The helicopters slice the air above. The mass moves south.

Hey! Skymatsky calls. Hey! Hey! He calls again and again. He falls to his knees and tears at the beach. The beach! The bloody stupid beach! He stands up again and starts toward his car. He knows where they'll go. He'll follow them. He'll catch up to them.

A hand clamps down on his shoulder. Shai Skymatsky? says the voice. Is that you, Shai Skymatsky?

Sir! Skymatsky salutes.

Skymatsky, says the rav aluf. The head of the army stands with his men off the beach in the bushes. Why don't you go home? Go home. We'll call you when we're finished.

They call out as he walks to his car, Give our regards to your old man, Skymatsky.

Skymatsky climbs in. The army can go fuck itself.

Skymatsky drives home. He rushes up the steps that lead to his apartment. He throws open the door but she's already gone.

Chapter 12

MARC IN HANDCUFFS

THE DETECTIVES ask him about gambling. They ask him about his secretary. Molly, his secretary, a tough paralegal from the Valley, argues with the police. She'd insisted on calling a lawyer. She's telling the detective they've made a mistake.

The rest of the company is up in arms. Some of his guys argue with the officers. The IT guys are asked to give the Dropbox password. You give us the password, we won't take the computers, says one of the detectives. Saul, one of his IT guys, looks over at Marc. Marc nods.

Give it to them, Marc says.

But they're making a pile of the computers anyway, against the objections of Saul, who finally slumps in his chair and submits to having his bag searched.

The police officers are emptying and rifling through the bags of the employees. They have large plastic bins in which they place laptops and tablets.

Marc is chai b'seret. Living in a movie.

We'll have to call in a truck, one detective calls to the other, to get all the computers.

The chief detective Gambello drifts in and out of Marc's office. Quite an operation, he says to Marc. Tell me. How do you afford this space? Rent alone, guys you got working here.

Financial services, Marc says. I told you. I run a successful financial services firm.

Oh right, Gambello says. You mentioned that. So what about the gambling? You know about the database in your cloud?

No, Marc says. I have no idea what you're talking about.

Some of your guys seem to think there was a pool—

Where isn't there one? Marc says. I'll bet even in your precinct—

Watch it, the detective says. Marc slumps in his chair. Gambello raises his finger up and darts it toward Marc's face. He calls out, All right. Take him in.

Two detectives come into Marc's office and pull Marc up out of his chair. They hold onto his arms, one on each side. The IT guy, Saul, says in Hebrew, We'll come for you.

Marc is led out the glass doors to the elevator bank. They turn him and he faces the office. One of the detectives presses the down button.

Marc says to the detective: Come on, take off the handcuffs. Don't take me down the elevator in handcuffs.

The detective sucks the air between his teeth. You think any of these people will remember? In a week they'll forget everything. No one remembers anything in this town, he says.

As the elevator doors close, Marc watches Molly through the glass windows as she bursts into tears.

The doormen stand and gawk as Marc is led through the lobby, one detective lightly holding each arm. Marc remembers when they rented the space in the building. They'd left New York for warmer weather and the beach. How Marc suffered those New York City winters and the commute into Wall Street. He dare not look down but he is afraid he will trip over his feet. Having his hands cuffed behind his back throws him off balance. He shuffles slightly, but dignity above all.

The police car waits out front. A cop leans up against the hood staring at his phone. They place him gently in the back-seat. Careful of your head, the cop says. Marc's eyes fill, this unexpected moment of kindness. Not kindness exactly, but consideration.

Sitting comfortably is impossible with his hands cuffed behind his back.

We'll take you down to the Metro Center, the cop driving says.

The detective turns to look at him. Just a few more minutes, the detective says. Sorry about the handcuffs.

Marc is pulled out of the car and led into the police sta-tion. LAPD. For Marc, it's surreal. He's sat on a bench and his handcuffs are removed. The detective sits beside him. Betcha never thought you'd be here, the detective says.

I've seen worse, Marc says.

Oh yeah?

Sure. Marc shrugs. The army.

Oh yeah, right. You guys all have to serve.

Marc nods.

Well, the detective says. I never served. I wanted to. My brothers served. My dad. You know. But I got a heart thing. Almost kept me out of the force. I been here twenty years.

Yeah? Marc says. Twenty years. Huh. Marc nods. That's a lot.

Sure. I'm all set to retire. And then. I don't know what I'm going to do. You guys in finance, you make pretty good money.

Marc thinks about Carolyn and the house in Santa Monica. He winces. Before the kids, everything they owned could fit in the back of a taxi. They had a tiny studio on the Upper West Side. Marc remembers how cold the winters were in New York.

Yeah, Marc says. We do all right.

Let me ask you. You got some advice? I got some money saved.

Marc is led into a room. They snap his mug shot and take his fingerprints. Make your phone call, they tell him. Marc feels around in his pocket. No, of course. They took his phone.

You got to make an account, they tell him. Whoever accepts the call pays ten dollars a minute so you're gonna wanna make it short.

Marc calls Saul. In Hebrew he tells him to empty the accounts, any accounts the police have not already got to. Saul sighs and tells him the accounts are frozen already. He quickly tells him the account number. He tells him he's going to need bail money. He's not sure how much but probably over one hundred thousand. They'll need to put ten percent down.

Everyone's gone home, Saul tells him.

Marc pinches the skin of his temples. Nu, ma? Marc says.

I'm not sure they're coming back, Marc. Ani mitsta'er. I'm sorry.

Saul, Marc says. We've known each other how many years? Eight years? I'll come back. You'll see. The firm will be back on its feet in no time.

I hope so, Saul says.

Get the money together. Call the bondsmen. I'll be in touch. Call Carolyn and make sure she's all right.

Another hour goes by. Marc sits beside the detective, who tells him his life story. His divorce. The troubles he's had with his older son. Marc is grateful for the company. After the second hour, he's given a stack of clothing, brought into a room. Asked to turn around while some poor bastard looks up his asshole.

He's handcuffed again, thrown into the back of a police car. The detective who's been babysitting him waves goodbye. The handcuffs chafe his skin. He's got a neck cramp. This time the cops drive fast with the lights on and he's thrown around the back of the car a bit and driven to police headquarters downtown.

Bail is set at one hundred fifty thousand and Marc finally sees the inside of a jail cell.

Hard benches line the walls. Twenty men sit and stand around the cell. The guards heckle him. I got a good business, Marc says.

Oh yeah? the guard says. He glances at the other guard and they exchange a look Marc can't quite decipher. You make a lot of money?

Sure. It's a good business.

Yeah see, says the other guard. You make a lot of money. That's why you over there on that side and we here, on this side.

The guards laugh. They high-five and Marc suddenly has a sense of himself. As *they* see him. A rich guy who got caught doing unsavory things. Doesn't it happen all the time? He sees how naïve he's been. Imagining they would understand his point of view. Recognize their mistake. That he's done nothing wrong. A gambling ring? In every office in America for every sporting event including figure skating, probably. Some office somewhere is gambling on a Little League game. How can this be? In America? How can this be?

A man approaches. He's dark-skinned with slicked-back hair and a handsome, youthful face. Hey, he says to Marc. How much your bail?

One hundred fifty thousand, Marc says. The size of the amount shocks the man, who Marc can see is really just a boy. Probably still in his teens.

Man, what did you do? the boys asks.

I didn't do anything, Marc says.

Yeah, the boy says. I didn't do anything either.

The other men in the cell crowd around Marc. They compare bail. They look to Marc for approval. All of them are innocent. One guy has not paid child support. He claims unemployment. Another guy is in for a bump of coke. He claims he was holding it for a friend. Armed robbery, domestic violence. Public lewdness. Everyone is innocent. One man whistles. That is a steep bail, he says to Marc.

Marc understands. Highest bail is king. He is king of the jail cell.

They ask him for advice about finance. Can he get them a job? Where is he from? What did he do in the army? No shit! they say. Commando! You like Rambo, they say. Their eyes grow big. How many Arabs you kill, they ask. Yeah right, they say, when he tells them none. It was peacetime, he says, when I served. The guards bring sandwiches in clear plastic wrappers. Bologna and cheese on white bread. Marc wolfs it down.

It is delicious.

Chapter 13

THE SOLDIER GABRIEL

STEP AWAY from the door, Joseph says in his biggest, most grown-up voice.

The weight against the door lessens and Joseph pushes it shut as hard as he can. Joseph turns the dead bolt.

The soldier begins to weep. Joseph sits down on the floor of the apartment. He is too stunned to cry. He stares at the floor. It is wooden parquet, newly installed.

The phone rings.

Joseph, please, the soldier whimpers. Please let me in.

No way, Joseph says under his breath. No way.

The weeping on the other side of the door grows louder and Joseph's stomach begins to growl. When he stands up, he is dizzy and slides back down to the floor. Shh, Joseph says, addressing the door. Shtok! Joseph says. Shut up!

I cannot, the soldier says. I am heartbroken and I have lost my way.

The phone stops ringing and Joseph crawls across the floor toward his bedroom. He will shut the door and pull the blankets up over him and by morning the man will be gone and the cafe will open. He will dress quickly and get himself a croissant. No, thinks Joseph. Do not think about the croissant. But it is too late. His stomach is growling and the man is pounding on the door again. He wails Joseph's name. But Joseph is halfway across the new living room floor that Saba Yakov put in as a consolation gift when he'd forced Joseph's mother to break up with her last boyfriend.

The soldier pounds on the door. He shouts, Joseph, Joseph! Ach sheli! My brother!

Joseph has no brother.

Clawing animal noises come from the other side of the door.

Allo? a voice shouts from deep in the stairwell. A woman's voice. The neighbor upstairs. Mi zeh po? the voice asks. Who's there?

Joseph springs to the door. He must shut up Mrs. Tzifat, who is a busybody and who will ask for Joseph's mother. Never mind, Mrs. Tzifat, Joseph says, calling through the door.

Joseph, is that you? Joseph Mendel? Is that you?

Yes, Mrs. Tzifat. I'm fine.

But who is there, Joseph? Who is making so much noise?

Never mind. It is just my cousin. He's come to visit.

Let me talk to your mother, Joseph.

Never mind!

The soldier calls out, It is okay, Mrs. Tzifat. It is only me, Gabriel Strauss. Don't you remember me?

Joseph opens the door quickly. Shut up! he whispers, furiously. The soldier pushes through the door with the butt of his gun.

Rabble-rousers! the old woman shouts down the stairs. They wait until Mrs. Tzifat's door closes. Joseph crouches down in the doorway between the apartment and the stairwell. Joseph could escape now. He could run all the way to his father's house. But somehow he is curious and no longer afraid.

The soldier wanders around the apartment. He stares at the bright new floors, the gleaming table, the invisible particles in the air. Joseph wonders what he is thinking. The soldier lingers by the stereo, shuffling through a pile of CDs. He selects one. This was my father's favorite, the soldier says, and Neil Young fills the room. Joseph stares down at the soldier's gun and duffle bag in a heap beside the door. I trust him, Joseph thinks. He is IDF and he is American.

But still: Please, Joseph says. Please don't kill me.

Relax, yeled, the soldier says, bending down now beside him. I only want to take all your money and food. Hara katan, he says affectionately. Little shit. I'm joking! You don't trust me? I'm your big brother! Gabriel! You have never heard of your father, Avi Strauss?

I have no big brother, Joseph says.

You have! Don't you know? The soldier throws his arms out in front of him as though to hug Joseph. Joseph backs away toward his bedroom.

You can stay on the couch, Joseph says to Gabriel. You can stay if you will be quiet. And you can go tomorrow.

Where is your mother? When is she coming back?

Joseph slumps. She's in Los Angeles, he says. She comes home the day after tomorrow.

Why are you alone?

I don't want to go to my father's, Joseph says. He doesn't want me. He has a new family now. You will have to leave tomorrow, Joseph says again.

Ah, you see, Joseph. That is the problem. I can't go anywhere. I'm stuck here. If I'm going to go anywhere, I'm going to need help.

What do you mean? Joseph asks. The soldier wears army fatigues. Black boots laced tightly up his calves. His large AK-47 lies on the parquet beside the door. Neil Young sings in English. Joseph hears the word "moon." The soldier speaks with an American accent but his Hebrew is good. What do you mean? Joseph asks again. You can go back to your army barracks. You have a place to go.

The soldier says, I'm not a soldier anymore. I've run away from the army.

Joseph shakes his head. It is unheard of for a soldier to run away. When you are caught, you are thrown in jail. Sometimes for months. In the end, your army conscription is not lessened, the months you were in jail are tacked on to the end of your service.

You must go back, Joseph says. Have you lost your head?

Yes, the soldier says. He begins to weep again. I've lost my head. It's back in Los Angeles where my mother and brothers are and my heart is, I think. Joseph. Will you help me find it? But I cannot go. I can't. It is unconscionable for me to remain.

Joseph sits quietly, stunned, watching the soldier weep. How do I know you are you? Joseph asks.

Your brother, you mean?

No, just you. The son of—the son of my mother's ex-boyfriend.

Avi Strauss was my father, the soldier says. He's dead now. The soldier pulls out an Israeli passport. He looks like a kid in the picture. Not much older than Joseph. "Gabriel Strauss" is the name on the passport.

I met your father once, Joseph says. He nods. Avi Strauss. He makes movies. My mother told me. I saw him in a café with his wife. My mother was furious and we left even without paying. Later, my cousins told me why. They said he was my father. He used to send birthday cards on my birthday, but my mother would throw them away. Sometimes there were checks inside.

Joseph feels exhilarated and also grown-up. Your mother sent my father Turkish coffee once, Gabriel says.

The soldier puts his identification away and picks up his gun.

What did you think of my father? the soldier asks.

He was fat, Joseph says. And your mother was old.

Did your mother ever talk about him?

No, Joseph says. But my cousins did. They call me Joey Strauss to tease me. How can you leave the army? Joseph asks. It will be difficult for you to get a job.

The soldier shrugs. Not in America. In America only poor people go into the army. I was going to be a professional soccer player. I was scouted and everything.

So what will you do? Joseph asks. How will you get back?

125

Let's go eat, okay, Joseph? What would you like? I have a little pocket money. I have a debit card and I think I have a little money left.

All the city is out on the streets. It is Thursday night, the weekend after all. A handful of people work on Fridays, but half-day only. Soldiers pass by, a whole clump of them, their AK-47s slung casually over their shoulders. Joseph feels safe with the soldier Gabriel. My brother, he thinks. He leans into him and Gabriel throws his arm around Joseph and pulls him close. Ach sheli! I have always wanted a little brother, the soldier says.

Everyone is loud and drunk at the pizzeria. Joseph orders two slices topped with sliced hard-boiled eggs. Gabriel orders plain cheese. Joseph shoves the pizza into his mouth. He is ravenous, so hungry that to chew the food is torture. He tries to swallow it whole. To inhale it. He eats the crusts too, slurps down his soda. Gabriel barely eats. Can I have yours as well? Joseph asks.

Betach, Gabriel says, shoving the half-eaten slice across the table.

They walk through the city together. The winds have started and the temperature begins to drop. Gabriel is visibly sweating through his fatigues. In fact, he smells bad.

Do you have a way to get back to America? Joseph asks. Can you call your mother?

Gabriel is silent for a moment and then shakes his head. I am ashamed. She might say no, and I cannot stay here.

Yes. Joseph commiserates. I can help you, Gabriel. I can help you. I can buy you a ticket home.

How?

Joseph reaches into the back pocket of his jeans. He pulls out his phone and pulls out a credit card. Here, he says. It is my Saba's. There is no limit.

Gabriel stops in the street. He puts his hands up. But I can't, he says.

Joseph keeps walking and calls over his shoulder, You can. You can order airline tickets from my computer. It is no trouble. I order food from the restaurant all the time. There is no limit and the delivery guy likes me.

Chapter 14

The Happy Couple

MARC SITS at the kitchen table and Carolyn stands. She is too agitated to sit. Carolyn is on the phone with the bank. Their accounts have been frozen and emptied. They are worried about checks bouncing and overdraft fees.

Their credit cards are worthless—such a loaded piece of plastic, Carolyn tells Marc. He doesn't look at her. Late the night before, she'd heard what sounded like a sob coming from his study. She'd tiptoed out of the kitchen and upstairs to bed. Carolyn says, There's no point in shredding them. Ours are identities no one would be interested in stealing. Carolyn laughs. For some reason I can't wait to tell my father, she says.

It will kill him, Marc says.

Yes, she says, and returns to the conversation on the phone with the bank.

The entire Solomon family will hear finally about Marc's arrest, through Marc's brother Dror and his wife. What's her name? Dror has already called and left messages on Marc's voice mail. Marc does not call him back.

We don't remember her name because she's a cunt, Carolyn tells Marc. She sets a cup of coffee in front of him. Carolyn is on fire. Your brother is a bit of a cunt too, she says.

Marc Solomon takes a sip. He shakes his head. Nathalie is the second wife, he says. We only remember the names of the first wives.

I wonder why they never had children, Carolyn says. Marc shrugs.

She empties the trash, lining the bags up at the kitchen door.

Carolyn never knew the first wife. But Marc remembers her well. The hot little cusit who later became a man, a *gay* man. Imagine that. Marc sets his phone on the kitchen table. Carolyn has gone to lie down.

The children have been complaining to him. Mom is always lying down. Mom doesn't feel well. Mom has a headache.

The lawyers call. There are three of them. They all talk at once. It is difficult for Marc to decipher what they are saying. He understands each individual word well enough but cannot put them together. There is no indictment. They have not charged him. The DA wants money, etcetera, etcetera. It will move to civil court. Civil forfeiture. They keep the money, you keep your hide. Pretty standard procedure in America. Try and get your money back and they will drag you in front of a grand jury. The lawyers, two of them ex–state prosecutors, tell him this is how police departments fund themselves these days. It could have been worse. You could have been in any other state other than

California where they can take all your money. In California they can take only a percentage if you have not been convicted of a crime. You will be able to keep your house provided you can get your firm up and running. You can refinance your house. Marc hangs up and the phone rings again. He answers it, speaks quietly. And the phone rings again.

In the afternoon, Carolyn gathers the boys to take them to their baseball games, their soccer practices. She will drop them off. She tells Marc she will be too ashamed to get out of the car.

But why? Marc nearly shouts. I haven't done anything! I haven't even been charged with a crime. In fact, the lawyers tell him he probably never will be. The DA could care less if an actual crime has been committed. He tried to explain this to Carolyn, who is paranoid. It was on the news, she says. It was in the newspaper.

It will die down, Marc says. Marc crosses the kitchen and opens the refrigerator. He must eat something. He hasn't eaten anything since yesterday.

Then why don't you fight it?

Marc looks defeated. Too much money in lawyer fees, too many newspaper articles. It's not worth it. All the lawyers say so.

The phone rings. Don't answer it, Carolyn says, and she hustles the boys out the back door to the garage. Marc watches out the window as they each climb, in their brightly colored uniforms, into their places in the Volvo station wagon. What a tasteful American family, Marc thinks. The car not ostentatious. The blond mother not too blond. The oldest blond child and the younger two a darker blond. The six-year-old wears brand-new cleats. Marc didn't have soccer shoes until he was sixteen years old. In the kibbutz he'd often played barefoot. How Marc would like to go to that place now. Just uproot everyone, abandon this sinking ship of his reputation and run away.

The car drives off and the clock in the living room, a giant grandfather clock that Carolyn inherited from one ancestor or another, chimes and ticks. The ticking gets to him. Time gets to him and he stands up and walks through the kitchen, through the living room to the clock. He opens its heavy glass door and stills the pendulum.

When he first met Carolyn, neither of them owned anything they cared about. They'd asked Carolyn's parents to hang onto the wedding gifts and moved out of their tiny Upper West Side apartment to Connecticut, packing everything they wanted in the back of their used Camry and leaving everything else on West 76th Street to be picked at by people. Carolyn was already four months pregnant, though they'd only been married one month. They'd been dating for five. This was before they'd decided to move to Los Angeles.

The phone rings.

We heard everything, Yakov Solomon shouts into the phone. Marc groans. Abba, how could you know?

Your stupid brother, hamor. What do you think? Ima wants to know if she should come. Should she come? How is Carolyn? She is very nervous. Carolyn is very tense. So tense! Ima is worried about the children. Should Ima come?

Carolyn is fine. The children don't know. We will be okay. Everything will be okay. I have good lawyers. I'm not going to jail.

Yakov whispers, Where is this Skymatsky boy? Dror told us everything! He says he fled the country with *your* money. Imagine! You hired your friend's brother! And then this. Nepotism never pays. I tell you! I've said it before, I've said it a hundred times. Your mother asks me why I don't find your brother Dror a better job. Well, now you see. Nepotism never pays. Never!

It will be fine. We are fine.

Talk to your mother!

No, Abba. I have calls coming in. I have to go.

Goodbye, Marchuk!

Marc hangs up the phone. He pads down the hallway and climbs the stairs to the master bedroom. Marc lies down on his side of the bed. He closes his eyes and for a few blessed moments . . .

Later, when the children have had their dinner and gone off to their rooms and their televisions, computers, and devices, Carolyn comes upstairs. She puts a pill in her mouth and swallows it with no water, a talent Marc has always marveled at.

She kisses Marc on the mouth. Do you want to? she asks. No, he shakes his head. By the time he gets it up she'll be a zombie.

Marc fingers the remote and finds a basketball game on mute. The television makes the dark room feel like it's underwater. Marc closes his eyes and remembers all those hours he spent underwater, in the army. It was a kind of terror but a manageable terror. A terror with borders. Carolyn arranges herself on the bed and falls asleep.

She sleeps beside him like the drugged and the damned. Her mouth hangs open. Her eyelids flutter. A tiny intake, a tiny rush of breath. The Xanax wraps its chains around her ankles and pulls.

The boys pass through to say good night. Good night, Abba. Good night, yeled. Good night, Abba. Good night, motek. Good night, Abba. Good night, heblon katan.

Marc thinks about his brother Dror.

This is a typical conversation between them:

My brother! Are you sitting down? Are you sure? Make sure you are sitting down. This is going to make your day! You really aren't going to believe what I have to tell you!

The sisters have spent X amount of money on Yakov's credit cards. Shira has been siphoning money from her savings to support an anarchist boyfriend *twenty years younger!* Her boy was left alone when she visited you in LA! The school found out and she was given a citation. She might lose custody! Did you hear? Ziv is moving back to haaretz with his boyfriend. They are going to live in Tel Aviv, in Shenkin! Abba will have a heart attack when he finds out! Guy Gever and Keren walk like somnambulant zombies all over the kibbutz. They say Guy has begun to drink. He lost another job. He's becoming religious. He's given up art. He's looking for someone to invest in a paintball facility on the kibbutz, of all things. He's spending a lot of time with Yoni Keret, who has become Orthodox and lives in poverty in a trailer with his *five girls* and one boy who is no doubt autistic; he left the army after just six months on *medical leave.* The younger girl is no longer religious and she is dating an Ethiopian! Can you imagine?

Everything recounted with a smile and a chuckle. Abject *glee.* Sometimes Dror can't restrain himself. He laughs until he chokes. It's a spectacle. There is horror in the world and no one can get enough of it and this is the trade Dror Solomon deals in.

Your brother, Carolyn has always said, is a terrible person.

My brother is a terrible person! Marc says aloud. Too loud.

Carolyn stirs, wakes up a little, rolls over and stares at the ceiling.

You never say anything bad about your family, she says.

My brother Dror does it for all of us, Marc says. He's already told my parents. That bastard. He gets up and leaves her in the bed to go sleep on the couch in his office.

The next day, Marc hears Carolyn come downstairs and grind a shot of espresso. The two younger boys are in the driveway playing basketball. Wind sweeps up from the ocean. There is a strong gust and the lights flicker. The clocks reset themselves to midnight.

Izaac, the oldest, is no doubt on his computer playing Minecraft, firing emails and texts to his friends and his cousin Joseph. Uploading videos to YouTube. Carolyn is barefoot and wearing loose yoga pants. Her ass is a shapeless mass of black Lycra. Since quitting her marketing job six months ago, she hardly gets dressed anymore. In the weeks since Marc's arrest, she hardly gets out of bed. Carolyn is in a kind of depression, or funk. She lights up dimly when the children come home from school and puts herself to bed just after they have fallen asleep, and sometimes before.

Marc Solomon sits at their kitchen table and watches Carolyn thumb through a magazine. He rubs his eyes until they are bloodshot. The skin around his eyes is purple and aged. He is worn-out, thinner. He'd been expanding and expanding all these years.

He contracts.

Carolyn, Marc says. Nothing has ever stuck to me. I've gotten away with everything and nothing has ever stuck.

Carolyn looks away. She sets the magazine down and stares at its cover.

Congratulations, she says. You have joined the human race.

Marc watches her fine, pale fingers. American. Protestant. Nervous. No lines on her white enameled face. Yet when she smiles her face shatters into lines. She has always been his beitzah kasheh: a hard-boiled egg.

Nothing sticks to the WASPs, he thinks.

I long for you, Carolyn, Marc says. I long for you every day.

Carolyn looks up at him. Her eyes cut him open. His bones are suddenly exposed. That's what he's always loved about her. The way she can cut him open with a look.

She says, You've been gone so long, Marc Solomon.

Later, the kids are watching a movie, sprawled across the couch in the living room. Upstairs, they lie beside each other and Carolyn remembers him, beneath the girth, the gray temples. White, wiry hairs poke out from under his shirt and stop at his clavicle. She *re-members* him. She puts him back together.

Marc wakes the next day and goes to his lawyer's office. For the time being, Marc's office is closed. They will reopen as soon as they can. In the meantime, the detectives have taken all his computers. The savings will dwindle. The firm will struggle to survive. Clients send panicked emails. Marc calls in favors, old friends from Wall Street, but it's difficult.

Carolyn makes phone calls and sets up interviews. She'll have to go back to work. She even calls her old boss, at the agency. But when she'd quit six months ago, she'd simply walked out. No explanation. It doesn't surprise her when her boss doesn't call her back. One day she and Marc will say to each other, *This is the best thing that has ever happened to us.* And tomorrow she will be old. The children will be grown. She and Marc will die.

These days, Carolyn looks at Marc and thinks: I hate him less. I hate him less and less each day.

Izaac logs onto his computer and tries to Skype his cousin Joseph. But his cousin is not online. Joseph is always online. He must be in the kibbutz or perhaps he's traveling with his mother. Of the three boys only Izaac knows everything about his father's crimes from the newspaper articles he has found online.

It is a secret he guards jealously. He's the only one of his brothers who knows. The secret is his alone.

Chapter 15

YAKOV IN YOUTH

WHEN YAKOV Solomon was born there was barely enough food for everyone to eat. His birth was not celebrated. His mother was already frail and nervous. Her milk did not come and Yakov the infant cried incessantly. She died soon after his birth. His older brothers, Ron Solomon especially, hoped Yakov would die. He was such a puny, pitiful thing and all the energy he had went into wailing. Only his father Shimon seemed to love him. He would dance around with Yakov in his arms and sing Hasidic songs to him, changing the words to Hebrew. This was the new land and Yiddish was forbidden. It was a relic of the Europe they left behind.

Later, Yakov's older brothers told him how their father cried at night for his dead wife.

The kibbutz was a raw factory of human survival. The men and women had come to Palestine after the pogrom at the turn of the last century with their communist ideas and little else. They were the new Jews. All money, resources, and food were pooled. No one had any more or less than anyone else. Everyone was ready to work. Marriage was an outdated concept in which the kibbutzim were uninterested. It was another custom left over from the old world. A relic. A superstition.

Yakov's parents had come from Bulgaria. Heavily influenced by Russian Jews, they brought their worn books of Trotsky. Religion was their history. On Yom Kippur, they ate sausage made from the wild boar that they hunted. They farmed the terrible land and worked hard. They pumped water out of the marshlands, which eradicated the mosquitoes and therefore malaria. Babies were born, got sick, and died. Sometimes women went crazy and sometimes the men. When life got too difficult for a few—due to drought, bad crops, fights with Arab neighbors—they left for the cities or went back to Europe. Some made their way to America.

They held their own civil and criminal courts, officiated by Yakov's father, Shimon Solomon, the most educated man in the region. He could read and write and speak classical Arabic. He could communicate with the local population. At times, the Bedouin in the region came to the elder Solomon to have their disputes mediated.

Born in Sofia, Bulgaria, Shimon Solomon was a largish man with broad shoulders. His nose was sharp and frequently peeled from the sun. He loved the Palestinian sun. It was different than in Europe—brighter and whiter. Not filtered through misery, upheaval, old hatreds.

The men of the kibbutz made a kind of peace with the Arabs. Before Yakov was born, Shimon Solomon was an officer in the Ottoman Army during the First World War. Shimon liked the Turks because there was always lamb shawarma. The Turks always had food. And the Turks liked him because he could read and write and knew the local population. He was captured by the British Indian Army after the Battle of Sharon and held prisoner for one year in Haifa. After the Turks were defeated, he was released. The British forced the kibbutzniks to get passports. They forced the unmarried couples to marry.

Yakov attended his uncle's wedding in Haifa with his cousins. The wedding was officiated by a red-faced British official. They'd traveled by bus to Haifa. The official spoke no Hebrew. The kibbutzniks spoke no English. Shimon was their translator. The Englishman wore very short pants. His legs were covered in insect bites. The Englishman scratched them constantly until they bled into his crisp white socks.

Around the time of the weddings in Haifa, Yakov, who was then eight years old, noticed a new woman hanging around the grounds. She was pretty and young. When the woman came around, Shimon would bloom. This new woman was from Berlin and she could read. She spoke other languages too, not just German and Hebrew. She spoke English with the British officials and translated their documents into Hebrew. Her skin was almost white, not brown and worn like the other women's. Her hair was blond, and hung loosely around her shoulders.

Yakov hated the new woman.

Please don't bring another woman to the house, Yakov told his father. I can do all the cleaning and cooking. Don't worry, Papa.

The woman's name was Gitel and she moved in the day she and Shimon were married. The elders said, What mazel. What luck! A mother, finally, for those five children.

Soon after, the beit yeladim was built, the children's house, and the younger Solomon boys were deposited there. Yakov and his closest brother, Ron, shared a cot. He was nine years old and Ron was fourteen.

After the class bar mitzvah, Yakov was chosen to go to the Balfour School in Jerusalem. It was a prestigious boarding school and an honor for Yakov. At the Balfour School, there was one building for Arabs and one for Jews. The Jews came from the wealthy families of Israel and some from Europe. These boys from the cities were studious and serious. Their hands were soft and their shoes were made from fine leather. Their socks were also very white and they never wore sandals, even in the hottest months.

Yakov didn't like to sit still. He preferred to work with his hands. He was penalized for going barefoot in the courtyard, for dirty shoes, for not showering, for not knowing the prayers for bread, the blessings for Shabbat. Yakov left the school at sixteen. He went off to the army but was discharged early for flat feet and bad vision. He was not unhappy. The army suited him as much as the boarding school. He preferred the land. He returned to the kibbutz and went to work in the brick factory. The Second World War came to pass, filtered through the tinny voices of the kibbutz-shared radio.

Yakov Solomon was now eighteen. It was 1947 and no one knew which way Israel would go. Like a boat righting itself, the country swayed to the Soviet side and then back to America. Yakov Solomon was enamored with America. He was a humanist. He was not a Jew. He was a man. He hitchhiked with his cousin Eli Solomon to Haifa where he meant to board a ship that would ultimately set sail for America. He loved America because he had decided that he was no longer a communist or even a socialist. He was a capitalist. He said to Eli, as they wandered through the near-demolished streets of Haifa: If everyone woke up each morning saying, how much work can I get done today, socialism works. But if they wake up, as they do in the kibbutz, and say, how little can I get away with, the whole thing fails. Eli Solomon nodded but Yakov could tell he didn't know what Yakov was talking about. Eli was interested in adventure, not ideas.

They wandered the seaports for three days searching for a ship they could find passage on. They were not the only ones. Many wanted to leave Israel now that it was no longer under British protection. No one knew, after all, if the country would be Jewish, Arab, or Christian. Soviet or American. Refugees wanted to go home, or to America where they had family.

Finally, their passage was procured. A crude oil ship left from Haifa. It would eventually take port in Liverpool, and from there on to America, or stay. They were to leave in six hours' time. They spent those hours drinking arak with young Arabs on the beach. Soon it was time to go. They got up to leave, to go back to their small hostel where they picked up their bags.

Later in his life, Yakov Solomon would wonder how his father and uncle found them. How astonishing that they appeared at their lodging and dragged them back to the kibbutz. Was Eli Solomon too afraid to go? Had he sent word about their whereabouts? Or was it Yakov himself, sending signals from some secret part of his soul, knowing he could never leave haaretz?

After the war, a new wave of immigrants brought fresh energy to the kibbutzim. Some of them were full of enthusiasm. They were true Zionists. They were willing to work hard.

But they were not as hardy as the first wave, the Poles, the Russians, the Ukrainians. These Arab Jews got sick more often. Everyone knew the Sephardim were not as hardy as the Ashkenazim. Worse, the women were literate and more beautiful than the kibbutz women. These Sephardim cooked spicy foods with spices they brought over in glass jars sealed with wax.

The Sephardic food, all the men agree, was much better than the Ashkenazi food. The Sephardic women were the most beautiful.

The women in Yakov's kibbutz were mostly Polish. They hated the Sephardic women. To humiliate them they deloused them with hoses and forced them to cut their thick black hair. They gave them new names and forbade them to speak French and Arabic.

On a terrible hot day in August, Yakov saw a woman, near the chicken houses, fighting with the kibbutz women. She cursed them in French under her breath. The Algerian woman would not let the kibbutzniks cut her hair. To the women of the kibbutz, she was an Arab. She said to them, in English, and then in

French, I am more clean than you! Look at you filthy women. Look at your dirty fingernails!

Phoot! Phoot! the Polish women said. They said this as though she were some kind of dybbuk, a demon, which in their eyes, she was. It was as though she had come to disturb the peace, this woman, this aravi. It came down to this: She refused. She said it again and again. Je refuse! Je refuse! And then in English: I refuse! The woman would not allow the delousing, the haircut, or the Hebrewized name. The other Algerian and Moroccan women stepped away from her. They wanted to fit into their new home. They wanted to keep the peace. This one had always been difficult, always seemed as though she looked down on them.

She was Vivienne Sarfati. She was beautiful and worldly. Later, they would say she looked just like Anouk Aimée, the actress. Vivienne had come to Palestine from Paris, where she was enrolled in the Sorbonne. She'd come to Paris via Algiers, where she'd lived with her father and mother and four sisters. She picked more apples than most of the men and cursed heroically in Arabic and French, and now Hebrew. She tied her shirt up under her bust and exposed a smooth, taut belly. She cut her pants into shorts. Her rear was heart-shaped. Her face was a perfect oval.

No, she didn't love him. No, she didn't want Yakov. She loved another boy. A boy from Algiers who had promised to follow her to Palestine, although, it was said, he was not even Jewish. Yakov paid Efraim Grenkel in the mail house to intercept the letters, but they were in French. Everyone watched Vivienne Sarfati stand outside the mail house with a letter to mail in her hand, wearing her brightest shade of French lipstick. She kissed the envelope. It was quite a show.

In the end, the boy from Algiers never came, not that Yakov was aware of anyway. Or perhaps he came and was turned away. If Vivienne was heartbroken, she did not show it.

During Sukkot, Yakov stole Vivienne away to the fields and tried to seduce her. I will never love you, Yakov Solomon! You are an arrogant, uneducated man, Vivienne told him.

Had there ever been a stronger intoxicant?

Vivienne's parents arrived a year after her and then, one by one, her sisters followed. Her sisters married quickly. They were all pretty women, the Sarfati clan, but Vivienne was the real beauty. She was going to Jerusalem to study business. Every day she left on the bus for class.

Yakov steered the kibbutz into the cement business. Soon after, with kibbutz funds, he bought construction equipment. Large cranes and cement mixers. They dwarfed the cowsheds and chicken houses. Cows and chickens, Yakov scoffed. What are we? A *shtetl*?

Yakov's older brother Ron was not happy with his younger brother's success in the kibbutz. Ron had never been happy. Worse, he'd fallen in love with Vivienne Sarfati too. He'd been seen mooning around the bus stop waiting for the evening bus from Jerusalem.

Yakov Solomon backed off. As the youngest Solomon, he was not meant to take on the leadership he had. He could not have the girl. Yet, there was something about the way Vivienne looked at him. Like she knew him. Even if he could not get the girl, he liked to be known.

And there were other women in the kibbutz, after all. This new generation was younger and smarter. They were better educated and more attractive too. Anyway, it was better not to mess with the Sephardim. They could crush the most fragile part of a man with their bare hands and never look back. They were not even Jewish, not really, but aravim, Arabic. If Ron ever got his hands on her, she'd ruin him.

Managing the kibbutz was not easy. Every day there were more headaches. Solving one headache brought ten more. The fish stank from the head, the old saying went. Any problems in the kibbutz were Yakov's problem, as he was now the head of the kibbutz.

The men came to Yakov to tell him about Shlomo Golani. Shlomo Golani had been stealing cows from the cowshed and slaughtering them. Men found a pile of bones smoldering out in the Valley. Shlomo took the meat for himself and his family. What are we going to do about Shlomo Golani?

What are *you* going to do about Shlomo Golani? Yakov's brother Ron asked him.

Yakov Solomon had been invited to the house of the sheikh in the nearby village of Saphsaphas. The village bloomed with red and white bougainvillea. The streets were swept. The elegant mud buildings squatted low. Everything was the same light brown color, everything but the flowers and bushes and the sky. A tiny child in a white smock squatted beside the door of the sheikh's house. She chattered happily to herself and to Yakov. Yakov pulled a tiny golden chick from his pocket and handed it to the child.

Yakov told the sheikh about this story of Shlomo Golani and the sheikh listened. He laughed out loud at the story of Golani, slaughtering cows behind his apartment in the middle of the night and taking the meat for himself.

Even his name, the sheikh said, is funny.

Yes, Yakov said. But what should I do?

But of course let him do what he is doing! Let him slaughter cows! The sheikh rose to his feet. Let him slaughter cows! If he does not slaughter cows he will slaughter people!

Months later, the sheikh came to the kibbutz office. He was stern and solemn. The sheikh had brought all his male relatives. His brother was angry and would not meet Yakov's eyes. They crowded the small office. Kibbutzniks milled anxiously in the yard out front. Yakov poured a glass of arak but the sheikh refused it. The brother also refused it. The brother asked Yakov, Haven't you people got enough of our land? The sheikh hushed him.

It is not we who want your land, Yakov said. It is them, and Yakov pointed north, south, east, and west.

They agreed in their meeting that there would be no fighting between the sheikh's village and the kibbutz. The Arabs of the village would not bear arms against the kibbutz and the kibbutz would not attack the village. Additionally, the kibbutz gave the sheikh six locally made Sten guns so the Arabs could protect themselves from the Jordanians, in the event they tried to raid Saphsaphas, the place of the willow trees.

Yakov Solomon explained to the sheikh that there would be gunfire at night. Do not be afraid, Yakov said.

Yakov told the sheikh to make shelters in the village. Dig in the ground large holes for the women and children, Yakov said. In the event there are bombs.

This, the sheikh refused to do. Our houses are so beautiful, he said. And they have stood two hundred years or more. Your concrete houses are so ugly. The sheikh spit on the ground. We cannot understand how the Jews live without beauty. The sheikh made a sign with his hands. Allah will protect us, the sheikh said. And He will protect you also.

The kibbutz prepared for the fight.

Syrians came from the Golan. Jordanians came from Jerusalem.

Half the kibbutz men went to Haifa and became soldiers. The rest protected the land. At night the men on watch listened to the jackals howling. There were tracers and flares and fighters overhead.

During the day, life went on as always. Kibbutzniks tended their gardens and fields and cows. Half of the chickens died from disease. Around them, Arab villages were abandoned.

During the day, the Arabs from Saphsaphas came to borrow the kibbutz tractor. For this they traded za'atar spices, olive oil, pitot.

Each night, a young Czech scholar who had studied in Jerusalem snuck off to the sheikh's village and translated for him the news from the Arab news service. For though the sheikh was a judge in the highest Arab courts, he was not fluent in the literary Arabic of the radio announcers.

A Transjordan Frontier Force checkpoint had been set up six kilometers down the road from the kibbutz. After the first night of shelling, these men disappeared. Yakov's brother Ron took over the checkpoint along with their cousin Eli Solomon and two other men.

It is at the checkpoint that Ron Solomon was killed. He was shot by Jordanians. Yakov was bereft. Vivienne felt no such sadness over her lost paramour. She thrived. She cut her hair short and gamine, like a movie star. She wore lipstick her mother brought her from Algiers. She came to Yakov wearing her scandalous red lips as he was walking to the building where they made bricks. She watched him clear out the chicken carcasses. She watched him all the time now and finally, she said to him, Now I'm free, Yakov Solomon.

Yakov Solomon hears the sheikh's brother had been killed. He'd gone off to fight for the Syrians. There had been an argument between the brothers. The sheikh had commanded him not to fight, but the brother was hotheaded and full of rage at the sabras and went anyway. He was the sheikh's only brother. The sheikh has only daughters. The sheikh's family would no longer rule the small village, once the sheikh died. This was a good thing, the villagers said. They'd protested his collaboration with the kibbutzniks and saw him as a traitor.

Yakov went to him, as his father, Shimon, would have. He brought three freshly killed and plucked hens. Yakov came as a man who has lost his brother, Ron Solomon. His cousin Eli Solomon led a female goat by a rope. They walked through the Jordan Valley fields to the dusty village on the hill. It was untouched by mortar and gunfire. The men took their shoes off at the door.

The sheikh sat on a low chair. His eyes burned brightly. So brightly it seemed they burned for two men, as though the sheikh had absorbed his own hotheaded brother.

We have come to pay our respects for your loss. I am so sorry—Yakov Solomon began. He bowed his head and stared at the straw mat beneath his bare feet.

For a moment the sheikh sat and didn't speak. The silence stretched. Yakov began to sweat. He was unsure what to do. He had heard about the villagers' hatred of the kibbutzniks. Yakov grew frightened. The goat was restless and bleated loudly. The sheikh raised his head. He kicked a stool that was beside him across the room into the wall: L'JahHanim! he said. To hell! Don't talk about it. It's in the past! *L'JahHanim!*

Yakov shook his head as he walked across the scrub and brush of the Jordan River Valley. The air was so hot and dry it feels combustible.

L'JahHanim!

Yakov and Vivienne married. They had children. Ziv, Keren, Dror, Shira, and finally Marc. Marc was not a proper name for a kibbutz boy, an Israeli. But Vivienne—who regretted at times that she chose Israel and did not stay in France—wanted a child with a French name. Anyway, she said, I am tired of naming children after bushes, trees, and acronyms, she said. Let this boy have a proper name. A name one could share with a boy in France, or America. Ziv, Keren, and Dror went off to the army and Yakov grew more powerful in the local councils. He created a construction company with a wealthy Druze man from Beit Jann. He and Vivienne stayed in their tiny apartment. They ate in the dining room like everyone else. His prestige grew. The money he earned went back to the kibbutz. He took a small salary, only. His old classmate from the Balfour School, Yitzhak Rabin, asked him to become the finance minister and he does this for four years, traveling to Jordan, Algeria, and Egypt. He was the guest of kings and prime ministers. He believed in two states. Only through commerce can we wage peace, he said to everyone who would listen, and for a short time it looked as though there would be peace.

And yet, around him the settlements grew with Yakov's cement and Yakov's equipment and Yakov was ashamed of them. It was one thing to buy land but another to take what does not belong to them. Meanwhile, the kibbutz was very rich. One of the few successful ones left in Israel. He kept his thoughts to himself as everyone around him talked of how Israel must continue, the Jews must go on, and he said to himself but never aloud: Ah, but why must the Jews go on? Are we not all men?

L'JahHanim!

Chapter 16

NAPOLEONIC CHÂTEAU

ALAN ATTAL is virile but old now. He is almost seventy. His denim is tight, not quite blue, not quite gray. The back pockets run down his backside in the new modern style. He pours glasses of cognac until the bottle is finished and then pours tequila. The men, the different generations of commandos, take wide seats in their beach chairs. Their legs outstretched, their chairs pulled away from one another. The Mediterranean crashes against the beach at Antalya in the Turkish Riviera. They are all drunk in their linen shirts and leather sandals. The wives are back in the rooms of the resort, not permitted to join the evening parliaments the ex-soldiers hold. Anyway, they've heard all the stories a thousand times before. They are bored of them.

Attal continues: The commanders tell me first to go to Jerusalem to get papers to leave for France. They tell me: Do not put on your passport you are from a kibbutz. Do not tell anyone your people are farmers. Say you are from the city. Say you are from a fashionable district in the city. That your father is a diplomat, a businessman, a university professor. Anything, please, but a farmer!

I ask, But why?

The commanders tell me: You are going to France. You are going there for one year to train. If they know you are farmers' children, they will have no respect for you.

This to me is unbelievable! In Israel, of course we are the best in the world, what does it matter what our fathers did? What is dishonorable about farming? But I am excited too, to go to France, and so I go to Jerusalem and a passport is made for me. I say my father is a lawyer. I was born in the Upper Galilee but I say I was born in Haifa.

We go to France because France is where the best diving equipment is made. Of course France, because since Jacques Cousteau, they own the sea. That is true. The technology of the sea, the French own. But what is really funny is that the French have not won a war since Napoleon. No, this is true. Think about it. And now I will tell you why.

First, we arrive, myself and two other officers plus six trainees, to a chalet in Toulon. The chalet is built about ten meters off a cliff with buttresses that go down to the sea to hold it up. It is quite a thing to behold! And very old. Maybe three centuries. It is, what can I say? It is a castle. This is where *twenty* officers live. Just twenty. Can you imagine?

Breakfast was to start at nine a.m., an unheard-of time. We'd all been up since five a.m. and so were very hungry and also a little confused. We wondered if it were not a French holiday? But no, it is like this every day. It took some getting used to.

Especially for us farmers, you see! We were led through a giant hall to an even bigger one. This second room was the dining room. There, the six officers sat around a large table. There were places set for us. Crystal goblets, silverware and napkins. You know, the whole works. We had been trained in our table manners before coming but had not expected to ever use this training! Three butlers came in and each of the French officers received three newspapers each. We officers were brought the *International Herald Tribune*, in English, which none of us could read. It was not a heavy breakfast, the French being French, you know, there was no salad and no eggs. Just nice baguettes and croissants and very good jam. A little cheese and really very bad coffee.

After breakfast we sat in the large hall on sofas and settees and talked about the mission we would have that evening. It was all going very well with the men when a bell was rung. It was eleven thirty, time for lunch. We were very happy as the breakfast had been so light—but delicious, you understand. I was the most junior and I watched the men around me. It was there that I learned the fabric napkin must be carefully placed on the lap and not tucked up into the shirt or left ignored on the table.

The men talked more at lunch. It was more casual, perhaps because of the wine. The officers would request, you know, an 1860s Château blah blah blah from their butlers, who would go down to the wine cellar and fetch it. They would order a bottle for us too. They were very generous. The butlers offered soup from silver tureens with silver ladles. The French spoke of their country estates, their peerages, their staffs, their families, and their cars. They asked us polite questions about our families and about Israel and we answered as best we could. The best families in Israel, as you well know, are from the farms and kibbutzim and I suspect the same is true for France, but those soldiers didn't see it that way. Still, they were all very nice to us.

Those French officers! You know. They haven't won a war since Napoleon! But, they *know* how to live.

After our two-hour lunch we took a rest. Rest! A menucha in the middle of the day! We Israelis had begun to relax into this new lifestyle. I couldn't believe I was to be here for one year. I'd left my wife back on the kibbutz at home and my two-year-old son too, so you know this was very difficult. After the rest, we discussed the evening operation. There was a long dinner with roast beef, many courses. Dark comes late in France. I don't know why this is so, but the summer light there is magnificent. We left for the operation at ten p.m. Truth be told, we were quite eager to get down to business. We are not used to doing so little. There was new equipment to try. We were eager to get into the sea.

The sea was warm and calm. There were some unexpected delays but we were used to it. We were surprised when the French began to pull back, saying, It's eleven o'clock. It was too late for them, you see. It was past their bedtime!

Those marvelous people!

The next day was parachuting day. In the army there, as here, you get compensated per jump. One day a week would be reserved for this. In Israel, of course we do this one time a month, maybe every two months. Not so in France. We flew up in those planes and jumped out, landing in a perfect field of fresh lavender. We were driven back to the airfield, where the plane was waiting for us, fueled and ready to go. Had we misunderstood something? No! We were to go up and jump again! We jumped with the men six more times that day; two of the French officers jumped twice more than that. This, you see, is how they raised their pay each month. It was extraordinary! My God—the fuel alone!

On Friday evening, the mistresses would come to visit. The wives and children were seen strictly on holidays. On Friday evenings, the men had dinner in their private chambers. We Israeli officers would eat together then and sing songs for Shabbat and get drunk on their fine wine and cognacs.

Those French officers! You know, the French Army has not won a war since Napoleon! Think about it. You'll see I'm right! World War I, World War II, Algeria, Vietnam . . . not one! But those French, they know how to live. You know who lives better than a French Navy commando? A Catholic bishop! No really, that was a joke they used to tell.

Best year of my life, that year in France.

The men move on to other stories. A waiter brings a bucket of Turkish beer and places it in the center of the circle. One of the men, a forty-year-old reservist, begins to tell the story of Shai Skymatsky, who stood in his underwear on the beach trying to flag down an entire operation at sea.

Chapter 17

THE END FOR YAKOV

THE EARTH is cold for all, in the end.

Yakov remembers the port in Haifa. He, a native-born sabra of Israel, the son of Bulgarian Zionists, was going to America. He had borrowed money from the old rabbi, who was wise enough to know the Jordan Valley was too small for Yakov Solomon. He was going to sail steerage from Haifa to New York. He had big dreams and they were not going to sizzle like a drop of water in the Kinneret in August. They would not evaporate into airless air.

For Yakov is sick. No one knows it and Yakov doesn't want to know it. But there it is. He can feel it.

He hobbles down the stairs of his house from his bedroom to his prized possession, a treadmill, hoists himself up and hits the on button. A little run and he'll be right as rain. He sets the pace, a bit higher than normal. How he must look to the young people with their red, sweaty faces and their flab. Like a stallion! When did young people get so fat? With the junk they eat and the hamburgers and French fries and cola, all the time drinking this terrible cola imported from America.

Yakov has lived well, eaten well, drunk well, fucked well. He'd created the biggest collective construction company in the whole country. They had contracts in Egypt, Morocco, and Jordan. He could dance on tables with an empty bottle of vodka on his head as strong and mighty as any Cossack. He'd plowed through secretaries and kibbutzniks, goddesses, angels, and shrews. He'd enjoyed every one.

Every one. And then there was Vivienne. Still to this day as beautiful as the day he married her. So beautiful and intelligent that when she'd first come to the kibbutz, she made the Ashkenazi mad with spite. Vivienne despised him now. That was true. But it was part of her and it was part of what he loved about her. For Vivienne knew Yakov. In all senses, he was known by her. It made him glad to think of Vivienne as he ran on the treadmill, faster and faster, his heart rate struggling to keep up with the extraordinary pace of his legs. He was so fit. His doctor couldn't believe it! So fit, he refused all medications. There is nothing in the world that cannot be cured with a salad before bed in lieu of dinner. It seemed to Yakov in that moment that he could outrun everything. He could outrun them all. His mother, dead now an impossible amount of time was waving to him, encouraging him to keep moving forward, and he ran and he ran toward her, his imaleh. There she was! Why, she'd been gone so long. He'd known her only from photographs. His legs were no longer beneath him, and in that brief but endless moment before his body hit the rubber track of the treadmill, he was flying.

Chapter 18

AT NIGHT YOU DIVE

HE WAKES up from a deep sleep to the sound of shouts. It is three a.m. and the night is moonless. They shout: Equipment. Deck. *Achshav!* Now. There are blows and curses. Bodies thud to the floor, pushed and kicked from their cots. It's winter and he can hear the rain on the plastic roof. Warm blankets are trampled on the cement floor.

He is pushed into a truck and driven to the port. He jumps from the truck with the rest of his unit. They pull on diving suits, still freezing wet from the morning practice. He curses the day he signed up. Right now, if he'd been smart, he could be the chauffeur for a general, sleeping soundly in an apartment in Tel Aviv. He could be in the Sinai smoking hash with the Bedouin, or even in the Jordan Valley in his kibbutz room sleeping off a night of heavy drinking. His powerful father had the connections to secure him any command he wanted. But instead, this: the slime from the port pushing bile into his esophagus.

He snaps his mask in place. Everyone around him does the same.

Finally, he lowers himself in off the side of the Kishon pier and watches the lights of Haifa. Longs for them. He longs for warm blankets and breakfasts. The yearning fills the vacuum until the dive is underway and then the fear comes. Water enters his suit at the neck, and runs down his back. He is grateful that his bladder is full. Later it will warm him. He sinks farther into the cold water, which is inky with oil that leaks from barges and ships. He can't see his hands in front of his face. All he sees is the glowing compass on his wrist. He can hardly make out his partner swimming beside him. The black shadows he sees in front of him are rats.

He reaches his hand up and searches for the metal of the ship. He smacks his head hard against the side of it and his teeth rattle. He understands he's between the mud and the metal hull. He must breathe—not too deeply—and relax the muscles in his shoulders. Fear is the water he swims in. If the fear gets the better of him, he will hyperventilate. This is how men drown.

Now he is out from under the ship. He checks the glowing watch on his right wrist, and the compass. He remembers the instructions: Kick south at a moderate pace for twenty minutes to locate the mark. He sets off fast and the kicking warms him. The twenty minutes pass quickly, the black interrupted only by the green glow of his diving watch. This marks him as a navy commando. The hull of the second ship looms before him; his skin senses the metal bulk of it. The device is strapped to his back. He reaches behind him and releases it. It attaches to the bottom of the ship with a satisfying thud. The magnetic component snaps it into place. First mark made.

Leave politics to the politicians.

He finds his way out from under the boat, careful not to let the current drive him into the sharp rocks that line the port, and sets off to the next mission. He sees nothing, only black water. He swims blindly and eventually realizes he is under a garbage barge, at least one hundred meters long and one hundred meters wide. He glances down at his compass to find his coordinates and discovers that the rust from the barge has caused a deviation in the compass. The needle spins wildly. His legs are numb; their movements begin to slow. He pisses into his wet suit to warm the lower half of his body. The Mediterranean Sea he spent his summers in is 17 degrees Celsius in winter, and the thin fabric of his wet suit does little to warm him. He waves his arm in front of his face in rapid motion, and the phosphorescence glows its phantasmal light. His partner, attached to him by rope, does the same.

He wonders if this is the end, then, since without a compass he will go around and around until the oxygen tank is empty, and search and rescue comes to find him. If he surfaces without completing the exercise he will be thrown out of training and sent back to basic to join the ordinary soldiers. He'd rather die. Out of five thousand who started the training there are only fifty left. But only twenty-five will finish. Twenty days remain, and he longs for that day when he will stand up in full uniform before the army commander, who will salute him and say, Good job, soldier.

Remember the guy in the unit before his who got lost beneath a garbage barge and ran out of oxygen and began to lose consciousness? Before he passed out, he saw a murky, underwater room with a man sitting in a wooden chair holding a candle. He was bragging when he told them this, and they all laughed and slapped his back. But Marc remembers the wild fear in the man's eyes when they resuscitated him.

He signals to Skymatsky through the phosphorescence and they agree on a direction. They may or may not be fucked now. They may or may not find their way out from under the barge. Marc's compass may or may not tell him the correct coordinates. He searches with his hands overhead for the rails of the barge, finds them, and starts moving. All they need is a straight line in a single direction and a slow breath.

As soon as Marc is out from under the barge, he checks his watch. He's been under twenty minutes. He has eight minutes of oxygen left, and fifteen minutes remain until their mission is finished. The compass strapped to Marc's other wrist finds north. He has forty strokes east to find his mark, but already there's too much CO_2 in the tank and he's started to breathe faster, his lungs hungry for oxygen. This is death for a diver and panic will only use up more oxygen. A good diver stays relaxed.

How are you? his mother, Vivienne, asks anxiously when she calls. She says if Marc isn't allowed home the next weekend she's going to call the commander of the army. He doesn't tell her what he tells everyone. I am broken. My dick is broken, which is the expression everyone uses to mean, I am at the end. I can't go on anymore. I'm finished. Instead Marc says, Everything is fine. I am fine. I have an extra day off for the holidays.

Breaths, like strokes, like meters, like everything else on a mission, are counted. Fast breaths are suicide. The powder that sucks the CO_2 from the breathing mechanism is too damp to filter. The carbon dioxide is recirculating and Marc begins to hyperventilate. Relax. Slow the breathing. Ignore your pounding heart. Divers have passed out from too much carbon dioxide, and drowned if they were not found in time.

When Marc completes his training, back home they will say he has a diamond on the underside of his dick. Marc dreams of the day he will go to Koh Phangan and sit on the sand and dry out his skin from these months of wet and cold. At night in his cot, just before sleep hurls its thick, black curtain across his consciousness, Marc dreams of the brown skin of teenage Thai girls that he has heard about from his older cousins. They bragged to him about how cheap the girls were.

Fifty feet in, Marc finds his mark. The click of the final device is the gladdest sound he'll hear all day. He holds the light while Skymatsky attaches the brick-like mine to the side of the ship with a heavy magnet. He begins to hold his breath now as they head back to the port.

Marc's mind takes in, in slow motion, the flailing of his arms and legs as a wave knocks him into a tiny cave, a hole in the rocks that line the port. He works hard to scramble out, before the next wave pushes him in deeper. He discovers that the cord that holds his gun to his chest is caught in the rocks. Marc can't get out. He has no more oxygen. He thinks: It happens like this sometimes. Skymatsky tugs three times on the rope attached to Marc's wrist. Tug back once. If Marc doesn't respond, he'll send up a flare and the boat will come and Marc will be pulled out. Who knows if he will still be conscious when the boat comes?

A month before, on a previous dive, the commander had called everyone in; the tide was too high. Everyone had returned except one man. From the boat the unit searched the water and around the reef all night for the soldier and his light, but the waves were wild, throwing men off their feet. A flare was fired, but instead of placing the flare gun on his shoulder, a rookie had set it down and thirty feet of flames shot out, taking his right hand off. The hand had been thrown one hundred feet into the sea. As the man was dragged screaming from the reef, the commander stopped all activities that night, and the next day Marc was the one who swam out and found the missing soldier's body, cold and smashed against the rocks.

Marc thinks about his current girlfriend, an officer. Will she mourn him? Or will she move on to the next promising soldier with a diamond on his dick?

Marc thinks about his ex-girlfriend Maya, back in the kibbutz. He's loved her on and off since they were kids and the kibbutz had tried to break them up, telling them they were too young. They'd carried on for a while after that, secretly, but he still carries a torch for her.

If Marc is lucky, he will be pulled from the sea and resuscitated. He will have the next day off and his weekend furlough will be secured—so long as he *stays underwater* right now. Marc imagines how he will tell this story to the officer, the one he likes to fuck with the shirt of her uniform still on, but unbuttoned to show her cleavage. Marc could cut his gun loose with the knife strapped to his ankle, but it would be an infraction—a lost gun—and any more of those and Marc will be sent back down the ranks, and that he can't let happen. He will humiliate the whole kibbutz. He will humiliate his father.

Marc works at the strap, but his fingers are useless. If he cuts the gun loose, the commander will ask Marc to wear his dress whites for a "talk." He's seen the men go up for their talk and never return again. But there's a chance he will live. For every death reported there are twenty men pulled safely out and left puking on a dock.

Skymatsky's face looms before Marc in the murk. He works the strap loose and sets Marc free from the rocks that held him.

Marc surfaces and clambers up over the dock to see another soldier in his unit. Y-y-okay? Eli Kaplan asks. Y-y-you were d-d-down there too long. Marc's heart warms and thuds heavily in his chest. Tick off this mission; there are only two hundred more such missions to go. The muscles in his chest relax. The muscles in his neck relax. The muscles around his knees relax to stop his legs from shaking.

The sun is rising behind the shipyards. Marc turns to the sergeant, who stands off to the side, a cigarette clamped hard in his jaws, and asks, What the fuck happened to him? He gestures to Kaplan.

Fucking rat fell on his head, just as he was climbing out, the sergeant says. He'll be okay in a few days. The sergeant laughs.

He strips off his equipment and suit and stands naked at the port, while Kaplan, who will never live down his rat fright, hoses Marc down. The water at the Kishon Port is radioactive from pollution. In twenty years Marc will receive a letter at his home in Los Angeles recommending that he have his head examined for brain tumors.

After four and a half years in the army he will be discharged. He will not take the position offered him in the Mossad but will travel instead to Koh Phangan to smoke hash on the beach and live in a tiny hut and sleep in a hammock. There will be nights when he will sweat out his dysentery. Later, Marc will visit the opium dens and take as a cautionary tale the emaciated men with their lips clamped tight around ancient brass pipes. His girlfriend, the officer—who now works at a mall kiosk in New Jersey—will call Marc frantically on the pay phone at a ratty local bar near the beach, the only number at which Marc can be reached. Desperate for attention, for love, for the promise of marriage. He will shoo the bar owner and refuse the officer girlfriend's calls. She wants to get married, she told him before he left. She thinks Marc is quite a catch and Marc is just cocky enough to think she's right, and just self-aware enough to know she's wrong. Besides, Marc loves Maya Frank. Would she be proud of him? It was his dream always to join Shayetet 13. Marc has heard reports she is moving to Amsterdam, or Copenhagen. She is an artist now. Marc has always wanted to go to Europe. On the beach in Koh Phangan, Marc resolves to go to Amsterdam when he is finished with the Far East and find Maya and marry her. Or he will move to America and become a millionaire.

Marc plays Frisbee, drops acid, and floats on his back in the sea. He grows his hair long and wooly and dreadlocked. His skin is as brown as the Ethiopians back home. He loses himself; forgets who he is and who he ever wanted to be. That person who wanted to be the person he wanted to be is gone now anyway. Thai girls with brown baby skin will pour coconut oil on his back and massage him on rickety cots set up on the beach. A screen around the cot means for two dollars more they'll give you a hand job. A man will drown and Marc will be the one to rush into the sea to pull his body out and try to resuscitate him while everyone around him panics. Marc realizes the man's not coming back and that he himself has turned to stone. He gives up trying to bring the dead man back to life and notices an empty bottle of one-and-a-half-dollar Mekhong whiskey stuck between the man's denim shorts and his terrible white skin. A crazed, stoned Frenchman performs mouth to mouth on the dead body over and over and over again. He picks up the dead man's legs and pumps them back and forth as Marc shouts at him, in English, This is not a cartoon, man.

Marc does ecstasy at three consecutive full-moon parties until the rains come and then he heads for Goa, where the beaches are filled with Israelis. The thick air sings with Hebrew and beautiful half-naked girls from Tel Aviv. There, Marc will lose his mind on mushrooms, and spend the next few weeks trying to find whatever it was that had once given him purpose. The propelling forward. The universe withholds something from Marc and it's up to him to find it again, that click, the sound of the mark found underwater as the device attaches to the ship. Marc will search forever to find it.

Over the years to come, he will work to forget that ceremony after surviving the four and a half years of training—the hardest training of almost any military in the world. But it will be difficult to forget how he felt that day in his pressed, white military uniform at the Western Wall. There was no war those four and a half years, Marc will say later to Americans when they ask. Thank God. It was meant to make him proud, his accomplishment. It was meant to fill him up and make him whole.

It is Marc's first lesson that no earthly thing can do that. Not the money and success that comes later: the university degrees, the blond American wife, or the German sports car that takes him downtown where he makes a million-dollars-a-year profit. He never forgets the cold sea spilling down the back of his wet suit. Marc's three blond American children will never understand his aversion to the sand and sea. His oldest son will tell him he'd rather give his passport back to the consulate than go into the army. Marc will agree. You're right, he will say. If we loved our children, would we send them to war? He will hit middle age when he wakes up from a dream in which he sees the general's face, his own white uniform, the way he felt nothing as the general shook his hand. That morning he will suddenly understand that the substance of ambition is only ever a shadow of what we thought we wanted.

Chapter 19

FUNERAL

EVERYONE IN the kibbutz dining room is tense. Vivienne, the widow, is stoic. She closes her eyes and she sees Yakov. All those breakfasts made. She remembers the years of Shabbat dinners, Pesachs, and birthdays. The little Hanukkah procession winding through the kibbutz with Yakov Solomon by her side. Vivienne had once been beautiful and, more important, she'd been good and where had that gotten her? She might have married someone else. She might still.

Guy Gever walks through the dining hall. He is animated. He is his old self again, only different, deeper somehow, and everyone is overjoyed to see him. It is said he is going to take money Keren has saved and the money they've inherited and that others have invested and open a paintball facility on the kibbutz. After all, he says, the splatter of paint on the trees and soil is an expression of art. The colors excite him. Keren's brother Ziv has promised a large sum of money. He is wiring it from Singapore. But Ziv is not coming to his father's funeral. No one has seen him in years.

Vivienne does not cry. Though she is heartbroken, as much for Ziv's absence and Marc's troubles as Yakov's death.

Vivienne's best friend, Aliza, and Aliza's neighbor Amos Solomon—Yakov's oldest living brother—stand nearby and argue about the pecan tree in their backyard. Aliza likes to make pecan pie. She is telling Amos that pecans are very healthy and they are preventive of many illnesses, like heart disease. She gestures toward Amos Solomon's belly. Look at you! she says. What? he asks, looking down. He is actually quite skinny, except for an abdomen that protrudes over his belted waist. Aliza gesticulates wildly, so animated she has forgotten they are at the funeral of her best friend's husband and that she is talking to the dead man's brother. One woman, a distant cousin, weeps alone at a table. Why anyone would cry for Yakov Solomon is beyond Aliza. He is not the kind of man you mourn for, he is a man you celebrate! Amos stands with his arms folded across his chest and juts out his chin. I am allergic to the pecans, he says. In another few weeks his eyes will be swollen and his nose will run nonstop. Aliza asks, Have you tried allergy medicine?

The family waits for Marc to arrive. They steal glances at the door, turning the direction of anyone new who enters the dining room, hoping it is him. They have all recently seen his picture in the newspaper. They have not seen him in person for so long. Some are surprised he still has all his hair.

Vivienne thinks Marc's hair is too long. He wears a beard now that shows gray hair and has a paunch. If only his wife, Carolyn, had taken care of him properly. He never would have aged so. Perhaps none of this would have happened, if not for America and that American wife. Perhaps Yakov would still be alive, if not for this American wife and Marc's problems over there.

The news of Marc looms large over the kibbutz. Will Carolyn come? Cold, frosty Carolyn. They feel sorry for Marc and sorry for Vivienne. To have a daughter-in-law like that. Not strong. Beautiful in a blond American way, but fragile. Never helps with the cooking or the washing up. How her hands shake at big gatherings. How she spaces out when everyone around is speaking. How terrible her Hebrew is, mixing tenses and gender. Not Jewish.

There is a large spread of food. Within ten minutes, it is decimated. Amos stands beside the empty plates and picks up crumbs with his wet finger. Empty trays are stacked with empty plates. Cups of soda are left to warm in the April heat.

The fans work hard. It is hotter than it should be at this time of the year. The cavernous room is hushed. The dining room was once the place where everyone ate three meals a day, excepting the Friday evening meal. Everyone but the very old ate the Shabbat meal at home. The dining room was built by a famous Russian architect, but no one can remember his name. Now it is the decaying symbol of a once thriving kibbutz. With its soaring 1950s buttresses, it looks like a Soviet airport terminal. It is rented out to the kibbutzniks for weddings and funerals and their Hanukkah parties.

Dror walks in with his wife, Nathalie, but Vivienne can't bear to look at him. Or her. They have driven in from Haifa, where they live now. This wife, the new wife, strides purposefully through the dining hall. She acts as though she already knows everyone. Nathalie walks over to Vivienne and greets her, hugging her tight. Vivienne stiffens. Nathalie speaks French to Vivienne, using the familiar. She is overly familiar and conspiratorial. She is not unsympathetic, but Vivienne distrusts her. They were both born in Algeria. Nathalie says she is also from Algiers, but Vivienne knows she is not from the city. Her accent is more aravi, Arabic. Nathalie is more likely from some smaller town. In Algiers, Vivienne had gone to French schools. Vivienne knows nothing about Algerian history or geography—she learned French and about France. She learned French history and literature, and about French cuisine. In the French schools, Vivienne learned to dress, modestly and with taste. She learned to stand and walk and sit. Nathalie wears four-inch heels. Her breasts are pushed up and out and revealed through the straining buttons of her blouse. Her perfume is loud and barely masks an odor of need, of greed, and famine. No, Nathalie and Vivienne are nothing alike.

And as for Dror. How can Vivienne forget the way he came to her and Yakov? Driving all the way to the kibbutz from Haifa and rushing into their house. The asinine grin lighting up his otherwise pinched face. So? Dror had asked. You sit here so calmly while your youngest son is in jail? You have not heard? You have not heard the news of Marc? So happy he could not hide his glee. Like a dog who brings a carcass to his owners and drops it at their feet. But the carcass was Marc.

Nathalie rests on a chair, alone. Her feet are swollen in her shoes. The kibbutzniks mill around her, the men's eyes flick over her.

Bolder men hold her gaze. She likes their flirting. But she's got a top dog: a Solomon. So don't even think about it, mister. All these women in ill-fitting T-shirts and athletic sandals. Would it kill them to dress up a little? The Solomons—the Ashkenazi, in general—don't know how to host a party. How much work Nathalie must do to keep things flowing nicely. She hasn't been there even an hour and already she's exhausted. But there is a good turnout, at least there is that. Dror talks to his uncle Amos. His hands in his pockets, Dror rocks from heel to toe, heel to toe. He is not the successful man Nathalie had imagined him to be. He carries the Solomon last name, but beyond that, he is impoverished. But still. There is a will and in just a few days' time it will be read. Everyone loved Yakov Solomon, it's true. But it is no secret he died a wealthy man.

It wasn't Dror who fucked up this time, Nathalie thinks with satisfaction. Even Dror can scarcely believe his good luck. Marc's prison tragedy. Marc's company shuttered. The American Solomons, penniless. It is sad but his father's death and his brother's troubles mean a new beginning for Dror Solomon. He can reinvent himself. He will no longer be in the shadow of his successful father. It was not Dror's disappointments that killed his father. It was his two brothers, the commandos, the money makers: one gay, the other jailed! And Dror was so lucky to have found Nathalie. He'd wandered through the wilderness until he'd stumbled upon this treasure. She would steer him onto the path of success. He didn't feel nearly fifty. He felt twenty, younger even! And Nathalie. She had taken all those self-help seminars and was bursting with wisdom!

Nathalie had dressed carefully, consulting her more conservative sisters. She'd toned down the cleavage. She'd worn slacks and lower heels and a cooler shade of lipstick. Leave the animal prints behind, they told her. These are Ashkenazi, her sister had said. And worse: kibbutzniks. They are plain. Wear dark blue. Wear black or cream.

She chose to wear black. Leopard only on her shoes and the muted print of her blouse. You would have to stand very close to distinguish the print of Nathalie Amsalem's blouse.

Chapter 20

THE RETURN

FAILURE SHOULD really kill you, Marc thought as he hustled off the plane. He would be late for the burial, and Yakov would never forgive him if Marc were late for Yakov's funeral. But permission from the DA's office was slow in coming and the flight he'd finally gotten on was three hours late, of course, out of LAX: third-world airport of the first world. Carolyn would arrive with the children tomorrow. His middle son, Sam, had the regional championship tonight.

Carolyn. Marc thought of her now and her yoga pants vortex. When she'd first quit the marketing firm job, he'd been angry she spent all her days in yoga pants and his old sweatshirts. But then they'd at least been clean. Now she wore and rewore the same pair. The same splotch of tomato sauce would get crusty and finally, by day five, just blend into the black spandex. It repulsed him. She didn't seem to understand that what had happened, had happened to *him*. Not her. And he had no time for the kind of depression she seemed to have fallen into.

The boys kept to their rooms. She seemed not to notice. Her eyes were bleary and swam in seas of Xanax. Marc wasn't sure she'd make it onto the plane tomorrow when she should be flying to Israel with the children. Izaac, the oldest, would get her there on time and packed with at least the essentials. They'd once flown to Israel when Izaac was eighteen months old. Carolyn had forgotten the diapers. You'll never forgive me for this, will you, Carolyn had said as they got off the airplane, disaster averted, laughing.

She was right. He never had.

Izaac had inherited Marc's good sense and Carolyn's straight blond hair. He wore it long. It hung thickly over his eyes. Izaac enjoyed the ritual of tossing it back off his forehead. He was good in school. He liked to skateboard at the skate park near the pier. He played video games and hated all team sports as a rule.

Sam and Nick, the younger two, had darker hair and Carolyn's blue eyes. The middle one, Sam, was ten and had Saba's nose and Marc's athleticism. The youngest, Nick, was six, and seemed to take after Carolyn's father with his rangy frame and broad forehead. Nick, as in, *just in the nick of time*, before they closed those doors forever. The mistake.

The plane landed. Marc pressed his temples with his fingers. He chewed on a nail and scratched at the hair on his face.

Marc walked through Ben Gurion to the car rental. He'd forgotten, as he always forgot, how obnoxious Israelis were. How they shoved and pushed and jostled their way through life. Always rushing, often shouting. He'd shed most, but not all, of those habits. Around him, men and women talked into their cell phones at all times at full volume. They formed a wall in front of the luggage carousel, not giving up an inch even as Marc struggled with his suitcase, finally ramming into a middle-aged woman, who cursed at him in Russian.

At Hertz, Marc stood in line. Three people ahead of him, an attractive young woman flirted with the clerk, angling for a discount. An old Moroccan couple sidled in line in front of him. Ma zeh? Marc asked. The old woman looked back at him and raised her eyebrows in innocence, the old man so sure of his place in the queue that he didn't bother to turn around. Hey, Marc said. He should curse them out. He knew the words, but it was like he'd forgotten the ways of this place.

But then, really, what did it matter? There were so many trans-gressions already. Marc sighed loudly. Almost a cry, and the old woman with her smudged lipstick turned to him and gripped his arm. She held on and swayed a bit, looked into his face, and then let go and stepped up to the counter with her husband.

Shira flew in from Los Angeles, where she had been visiting her boyfriend, Michael, and finalizing the details of what could potentially be a game-changing film shoot. She fetched Joseph from his father's. She was still furious with Joseph's father for not knowing Joseph was alone. She could not think about Joseph being alone without her hands shaking, and she has begun to take Clonex for her nerves. *What a boy!* her father, Yakov, had said just before he'd died. What a boy, he'd said, like it was a blessing, what a boy to stay alone all these days! *Maniac!*

She had a lot to think about on the train anyway. Joseph sat beside her, loud music crackling tinnily from the headphones screwed into his ears. She has fallen out of love with Michael. She met someone new on the airplane from her layover in Newark. At the El Al ticket counter, she'd been recognized and upgraded to first class. The man was younger than her by a decade or more, but ageless. He loved Shira's plumpness. He loved her on the Israeli show *Haverim*, from fifteen years ago. He watched the old episodes on YouTube. He cupped her ass and said, How can we make this bigger? And for that, she'd blown him in the airplane bathroom.

When he was alone, Joseph cried for Saba. He wept about missing his mother who had recently been on another traveling jag. He longed for that moment when she'd returned after his time alone in the apartment. How kind she'd been, and apologetic, and loving. Where was that ima? He had been living mostly with his father these days and he missed her and the freedom of the apartment in the Moshava. He wept for his brother, Gabriel, who the family says was not really his brother and was now in jail being evaluated for something called mental competency. He sat alone in front of his computer. On top of everything else, he was going to miss an important soccer match for his grandfather's funeral. His cousin Izaac Skyped him from America and Joseph answered. Izaac said, in his American-accented Hebrew, Don't worry, my brother. I am coming to you. Don't worry, my brother, Izaac said. Don't be sad. Saba lived a good, long life.

The cousins told Joseph they are all rich now. None of them would ever need to work again. Saba had probably left them each a million shekels. Look at all the construction projects with Saba's name on them, they told Joseph. They talked excitedly of the things they would buy until Keren came to scold them.

But the funeral was today, and Izaac had not yet arrived. Joseph's mother told him they would come the next day and stay in the kibbutz with them. His father had clapped him on the shoulder before his mother picked him up. He'd given Joseph his own white kippa to wear on his head.

Aren't you going too, Abba?

Ha! Abba snorted. That old man, *Yakov Solomon,* hated me on sight, and vice versa. But—Joseph's father caught himself—he was a good saba, Joseph.

Joseph's stepmother was skittish and shy with Joseph. She ignored him until it was time for his mother to get him. As he started out the door, she grabbed his wrist and pulled him to her. She was so unlike Joseph's mother. She was short and plain and she pressed Joseph into her breasts. She was not wearing a bra and one nipple was wet with milk from the baby. Joseph fought the instinct to hug her back, to hold onto her, in fact, as though he were drowning in the sea. He didn't want to be disloyal to his mother. If he were to love this woman a little more, it could only result in his own mother loving him a little less. And Joseph loved his mother so fiercely.

Chapter 21

Maya and the Sea

MAYA, DIVORCED from Levi Cohen, is now married to Shai Skymatsky. She washes the floor of her apartment by the sea. She brings out the bucket and the mop and splashes the warm sudsy water as she scrubs. She is barefoot and the feel of the water on her toes brings her instantly back to her mother's apartment in the kibbutz. How she washed the floor every Friday morning while her mother cooked Shabbat dinner. The long rubber blade she cleaned the floor with. The dark gray water pushed out the front door, leaving the clean floor behind. She sends more dirty water skidding across the white tiles to the tiny balcony that looks out at the sea. From the edge of the balcony, she sees her husband, Shai, on the beach across the road. He is frowning down at the phone as he makes his way barefoot across the sand. He calls something to her but the wind whips the sound out of his mouth. Ma? she calls. What is it? He shouts again. The waves crash.

She is so prone to these moments now, when she is instantly transported to an earlier time, or a future place, while at the

same time she is rooted *here*: Shai calling to her. Her feet wet
and warm on the cool tile floor. The wind from the sea shakes
the blinds on her balcony door. There is a baby in her belly. She
places her hand there and says, Remember this, baby. Remember
this moment.

Shai trudges through the sand. He's swum ten kilometers out
to the ruins of Yaffo and back, going along the shore just out
of reach of the riptide. His wife is so beautiful, so lovely on
the balcony with the mop in her hand. She wears only a T-shirt
and panties, and her four-months-pregnant belly is just beginning to show. She looks better than she ever has. Shai tells her
she looks like a teenager, just like she did when he first met
her, when she was still Marc Solomon's girl. Of course she is
getting on in age, already forty, but the doctor says everything
will be all right. Everyone had said Shai Skymatsky would not
marry! Would not father children! But look. Everyone should
look at him now.

The lights in the room could be blazing and Shai Skymatsky
will fuck all night long! His pregnant wife from behind, her
creamy Ashkenazi ass, spreading now with each passing week of
pregnancy. Now your fetus is the size of a grape, now a walnut.
Now your ass is the size of a young girl's ass, now a heavy girl's,
and now: ballooning to epic proportions! I love your big white
ass! he'd called out, and she had turned and gotten up off her
elbows and smacked him across the mouth, her ring catching
his lip and blood crimson on the sheets.

How he loves that woman!

Maya has heard about Yakov Solomon. Everyone has, of course. An article about his memorial service was on the front page of *Yedioth Ahronot*.

A real sabra, born in Israel seventy-five years ago. He'd gone to school with Rabin, supped with Barak, was the guest of the kings of Jordan and Morocco. Maya remembers him well. He flirted with her sometimes when she'd come to visit with Marc. He'd make her his famous salad. There had been a rumor about Maya's mother and Yakov Solomon. There had been a rumor about Yakov Solomon and every halfway attractive woman in the kibbutz, and quite a few of the unattractive ones. The funeral is Saturday night. Shai plans to attend, of course. Marc Solomon was his best friend from the army. He asks Maya to go, you must go! he exhorts, but she refuses. No.

But why?

Maya shrugs. It does no good to tell him and Maya has made a promise to herself she will not lie. It is not just her suicide attempts in the kibbutz, the failures and breakdowns, although that is no doubt what Shai thinks. The truth is, if she sees Marc Solomon, perfect Marc Solomon, she will not be able to bear Shai Skymatsky any longer. All the love she has for this good man who treats her so tenderly will drain away. Her heart will rattle with the dried seeds inside it and her life, as she now knows it, will hold no interest for her. Marc will be perfect as always and Shai Skymatsky will have food stains down the front of his shirt. Shai Skymatsky, a commando's joke: a great soldier, but as a human being, a mess. These days he makes good money

185

driving dignitaries around. A glorified chauffeur. A bodyguard. He is happy and Maya is happy for him.

Shai stands outside on the hot August pavement washing his tiny red Toyota. He wears his ratty red shorts. His brown belly hangs out over them, tanned, smooth, leathery. He waves at her. It's already starting. This man she loves looks different. Just thinking about Marc casts a shadow over him. He turns and sets the bucket of water down and his back is covered in black hair, like the pelt of a seal. Then he is bounding to her, opening the door of their apartment. The shock of the heat. She falls into his arms.

In the kitchen, Shai prepares food. Hummus with olive oil and sprinkled with paprika. There are good pitot. Shai toasts the pitot in the oven and the apartment smells of baking bread.

He asks how she feels. He tells her, again, that he will be going north for old man Solomon's funeral. He tells her again that she should come and reconnect with old friends and maybe see her mother, whom she hasn't seen since the last time she was in the hospital. Wouldn't you like to see Marc? he asks. He will be coming from LA for the funeral. Maya shrugs.

But you were once very close, Shai says. He has always been careful not to mention Marc around Maya. She has never mentioned him.

Yes and no, she says carefully. We were told by the elders we were not allowed to date, I don't know why. I think they thought I was too fragile for Marc Solomon. That he might crush me, and so they broke us up. We snuck around in the kibbutz until he went into the army. Everyone dates everyone in the kibbutz, Maya says. It is a small dating pool.

With what has happened to Marc, he needs all the friends he can get.

But what has happened to Marc Solomon? she asks. Only that his father died, yes?

Haven't you heard?

Chapter 22

VIVIENNE

VIVIENNE FINALLY sits down in a chair. Those old plastic chairs in the cheder ochel! Countless meals she spent in the old dining room before it was closed. How sad now that the cheder ochel is used only for occasions like these. A memorial, a party at Hanukkah. A winter wedding. She tries to avoid the large poster board with a photo of Yakov set up on an easel. It was taken not long ago at a birthday party for Guy Gever. She nurses a cup of seltzer water and watches Shira with her young son, Joseph. Shira is stiff with her son, awkward, as though they were merely acquaintances. But Vivienne remembers. That's how it is just before the bar mitzvah. The children grow up and become strangers. If the mother is lucky, the child will return to his mother a man.

Soon Marc will arrive.

Her throat catches. Vivienne stifles a sob. All the years she wasted on Yakov Solomon's bombastic nonsense. His stupid nationalism. Zionism. Communism. Socialism. Then a full embrace of capitalism. He died a rich man once the kibbutz was privatized. Doling his money out little by little. Ruining each and every one of them except Marc, who'd gone and ruined himself. And Ziv who wasn't here. The fighting would begin soon, any minute now, for whatever money he'd left.

Yakov and the over-the-top sabra shtick. Dancing on tables with empty bottles of vodka on his head like Zorba! Cavorting with all manner of women: secretaries—*armies* of secretaries— teachers of his children, wives of his friends, *her* friends. She was certain he would drop dead over one of them, plugging away as he had when she still let him. Doing laundry she'd fish out from his pockets those little blue Viagra pills, the little pilules his doctor had given him. Now and again she confronted him when she could no longer contain her irritation, and then his answers amused her. He'd told her Viagra was a workout pill for his "organ" to keep the "circulation" going since they so rarely had sex anymore. She'd told Aliza and they'd laughed and laughed. She was not altogether certain Aliza didn't count in that number. She was not altogether certain that other children of Yakov wouldn't show up at the funeral here in the dining hall. Certainly at the reading of the will. When she'd got the call about Yakov's collapse on the treadmill she'd called the attorney right away, before she'd made any other arrangements. The attorney was an old friend, living in town. Will there be any surprises? she'd asked.

I'm not at liberty to say, he'd told her, clearing his throat.

Vivienne wasn't stupid. Of course the children loved him, but everyone knew about the will and that there was money coming. Everyone remembered what Yakov used to say:

"Keep the milk close to keep the kittens closer."

✶   ✶   ✶

Vivienne watches Joseph trying to get his mother's attention. Shira taps into her cell phone. The dining room is too loud. The lights too bright overhead and the fans too sluggish. Vivienne is getting a headache. When will she be permitted to slip away to go home finally and sit in her empty house? She's been waiting for that day now for over fifty years. Shira tap-taps at her little screen. Vivienne crosses her legs and winds her hands together. We should marry our phones, Vivienne says out loud to no one. Maybe then we'd all be happier.

Marc finally arrives. Vivienne is overjoyed to see him. It is hard to believe he is late. He has never been late. Even his birth was to the minute on his due date. Initially, everyone hangs back from him. But then he is surrounded, consumed by friends. The dining room is filled with light from the early afternoon sun. Someone goes to shut the blinds and when the room is darker, they come and surround Marc, to shake his hand. To hug him, to be close. Marc has always had this effect on everyone in the kibbutz. He never should have left.

The freeway is full of traffic. Their car hardly moves. They are on their way to LAX. The boys, in back, listen to their headphones and play video games on their phones. Carolyn is mentally checking her suitcase. Has she remembered to bring a white blouse? Will the boys' good trousers still fit them? What about their shoes? She knows it doesn't matter much what they wear. Israelis have no sense at all of ceremony. She remembers the little band of Marc's friends who'd shown up at her wedding. They'd worn shorts and Tevas. Her mother had nearly had a heart attack. Would it kill them to wear a shirt with buttons? Never mind a tie.

Carolyn thinks of Yakov. It's impossible to believe he is dead. Her fists ball up and her fingernails dig into her palms. In the middle of all *this*, Yakov had to go and die. Marc will disintegrate, Carolyn fears. There will be such a fight for the money that there will surely be nothing left. Marc will walk away from it all without a dime, if she knows Marc. The youngest child. The peacemaker. She remembers the Xanax she carries in her bag.

Carolyn thinks about money. She'll have to buy the boys food at the airport, snacks and water and maybe a toy for Nick, but she's not sure if her credit card will work or if it has been canceled. There are only two modes of being in this world. You are either alive and well or your credit cards don't work and your bank accounts have been cleared out.

The youngest two, Sam and Nick, are surprisingly subdued. Yakov had once convinced them he could kill lions with his bare hands and was therefore immortal. Nick still believes this, as he still believes in the tooth fairy and Santa Claus. Sam, two years older, isn't sure about Santa Claus—but why does Santa Claus not come to the other children in Hebrew school? Izaac believes in nothing. Carolyn watches Izaac in despair. Is it puberty or is it normal to be furious all the time?

The night before, after packing the two suitcases and the duffel bag, a feeling had come over Carolyn, an ache in the hollow of her chest that's still there. Or no, not an ache. Something more neutral. A sensation. It is the feeling she has for her husband. How much she loves him, and at the same time, how little. Once upon a time, this no-name sensation filled her with panic or dread. But last night, moving through the quiet and stillness of the house, the children sleeping in their beds, she held the sensation as easily as one palms an apple, a pear.

The feeling comes and goes. Dissolved by her careful, neutral attention. Disposed of, and forgotten, she had curled up with six-year-old Nick, who had appeared by the side of her bed.

Vivienne sleeps alone tonight. Before the walk to the grave site, she'd tried to help clean up the cheder ochel but had been sent away. We will clean it later, her friend had said, after we walk to the grave. They follow the truck with the coffin of Yakov Solomon through the kibbutz to the graveyard, where they stand around the site, and throw dirt inside the grave on top of the coffin. Everyone places a stone on the heaped soil. People begin to wander off, nodding at Vivienne, Keren, Shira, Marc, and Dror, who goes back tomorrow for a business meeting in Tel Aviv and to pick up Carolyn from Ben Gurion Airport for shiva. In one year they will return to the site and place the gravestone. Vivienne looks at her watch. The sun is setting and the Jordan Valley cools. Yakov would say, *Now* the party begins! Now that you have all left.

So tonight the joke is on Yakov. Wherever that joke came from, it will likely never be told again. But in her head, though she loved him, tonight as she climbs into bed, she will say to herself:

Now that you have left, Yakov Solomon, the party can finally begin!

They will sit shiva, the will will finally be read, and Yakov Solomon, who once loomed so large, will start to fade.

Chapter 23

Maya and Marc in Youth

The problem with the romance between Maya and Marc was not that they were too young, as some had speculated. They were thirteen and fifteen, respectively. Nor was it that Marc often acted indifferent to Maya, though he loved her achingly in a way he has never loved anyone since. Nor was it true that Maya was fragile emotionally. The problem was not so simple and for many years, it was a secret.

Maya had loved Marc. She was the most beautiful girl in the kibbutz, with wavy light brown hair, a compact body and narrow hips and in her bathing suit: perfect small breasts. She didn't mind how Marc seemed one day to love her passionately and then ignored her sometimes for three or four days at a time. She didn't mind because it was far superior to how the other boys treated her, often with slavish, tongue-tied devotion that annoyed her. She acted just as indifferent to Marc as he did to her and it drove him wild.

Marc was the most handsome, charming, and talented of the kibbutz boys and it was only a matter of time before they would get together. None of the other kids begrudged their romance.

It was Maya who took Marc's virginity just after her four-teenth birthday. Marc was strong and cocky, but deeply shy. He'd hit puberty somewhat late. Maya understood that when he could not look at her in the disco it was because of his shyness and immaturity and his unwillingness to show his love for her in front of his boorish and unevolved friends. They'd done it first during the Shavuot festival, when the children spent the night in the fields. The youngest children followed the slightly older ones as they tramped through the fields. The teenagers lit bonfires and fucked in the brush. Sometimes unlucky small children would stumble upon them rutting away. Maya had brought a blanket and laid it down beneath a weeping willow tree. His friends had jumped out at them, laughing, and Marc told them to fuck off already.

She took him in her hand until he came. They crushed their lips together and she caught his ear in her teeth, whispering, Put this on, and handed him a condom.

It had taken only a few seconds. She was lifting up her shirt and showing her naked breasts, the small perfect nipples, and he was leaning over her with his cock in his hand, and then collapsing in dizziness and exhaustion. It wasn't more than a minute before she reached for him again.

Because by thirteen the children had their own apartments, she would show up in his room after his roommate had gone to the showers. He would wake up with her astride him, her hand pulling his hand to her breast, showing him that she liked her nipples squeezed. She liked a thumb on her clitoris while she worked over him. He liked her nipple in his mouth.

She came to every one of his soccer games. He admired her strange drawings. She could draw anything, true to life, like a photograph, but she preferred things that were more surreal. She would console him when Beitar Jerusalem lost. He would console her when her mother said yet another cruel thing to her. Maya's mother seemed to despise her. Maya didn't tell her anything. Did not tell her about her romance with Marc.

It didn't take long for the grown-ups who oversaw their apartments to get wind of their relationship. It would have to be stopped. No one in their group of friends could understand why. They were meant for one another! Plenty of kids were getting together, having sex in the field or even in their own beds. But no. This was different. None of the kids knew the reasons, just that they were each sat down separately and told they weren't allowed to see each other anymore. As it turned out, and few people knew—only Maya's mother and uncle and Yakov, of course—but Maya and Marc were brother and sister.

Maya spent the summer in Amsterdam at an art camp and came back with jet-black dreadlocked hair and a nose ring. She had utter contempt for everyone in the kibbutz after that and returned to Amsterdam the moment she finished the army. She was going to be a famous painter. She had a Dutch passport from her grandmother, who died in the camps.

Marc cried for six months when she left. He cried at night, but his roommate, who was his longtime best friend, didn't tell anyone and pretended not to hear. In fact, one night, after they'd broken into the kibbutz disco and stolen a bottle of cheap vodka, they cried together. Marc was devastated and did not fall in love with anyone else until many years had passed. Twenty years, in fact, when he met Carolyn.

There were rumors, of course, about their parentage. There were always rumors, as there were rumors about everyone in the kibbutz. Hardly anyone paid attention.

Chapter 24

KADIMA

K EREN COMES and throws open the doors and windows. She pulls the cloths from off the mirrors. Her mother, Vivienne, seems to have sunken into grief. A grief not even Vivienne understands.

Keren also can't understand her mother's sadness. Yes, Keren Gever loved her father. They all loved their father. But as a husband, he was lousy. He wasn't such a great father either. Look at how the children turned out. Dror, who handed his balls to his first wife and has not seen them since. Shira, who abandons her child. Keren and Guy. Only Marc escaped, and look what happened to Marc. Ziv has not returned. Now, of course, there will be money for everyone. Vivienne had always complained she'd rather be in Paris, or America. Now she can go! What is holding her here? She is nearly seventy-five, yes, but she is a young seventy-five.

Keren busies herself putting bottles of Coca-Cola into the freezer so they will be chilled before people arrive. She arranges salads on plates. Turns on the oven to toast the pitot. Who will come, Keren doesn't know. She posts to Facebook, checks her phone, texts some friends.

Everyone is welcome at the house for the next seven days. It is customary. Everyone is invited. Vivienne is against it. She wants to skip the whole thing altogether. Imagine sitting shiva for a communist? But Keren insists. He wasn't a communist when he died, she says.

He wasn't religious, either, Vivienne says.

Amos Solomon, Yakov's only living brother, is in charge of beverages and he comes through Vivienne's front door bearing two bottles of cheap lemonade from the kol-bo. The bells that hang from the door handle chime wildly. Keren takes the bottles from him and kisses his cheek: Two, Dod Amos? You only bring two bottles?

What? he asks, bewildered.

There are fifty people coming at least! she says. She'll have to send someone to buy more. Perhaps Dror, when he comes.

Amos Solomon is contrite. It wasn't easy, after all, being the older brother of a man like Yakov Solomon. Do they want him to go into minus for Yakov's funeral? He will not inherit Yakov's money, but Keren will!

Keren has no idea how many people are coming, or if anyone will come at all. Keren walks into the kitchen. She begins to pull bottles of soda and juice out of Vivienne's refrigerator. She pulls out a bottle of vodka, a bottle of good whiskey. Vivienne is aghast. That is expensive alcohol, she says. At a shiva! Mon Dieu. She clutches her chest.

Never mind, Ima. You don't drink anyway. I will send Dror later to buy more, Keren says.

Vivienne says, I might start drinking now.

Keren rolls her eyes and curses under her breath. Amos sits beside the kitchen table, beside the plates of hummus and eggplant salads, the pickled beets, the fennel, the pitot hot from the oven. Keren finds the good white Pesach tablecloth and arranges the plates.

Guy Gever is quiet today. Yakov had been like a father to him. Keren looks over at him and is flooded with love. Guy catches Keren looking at him, and smiles. A real smile. How she loves him.

Dod Amos pours himself another glass of his dead brother's whiskey. You died before me, you old bastard, he thinks. Keren sets out napkins. The phone rings and Vivienne rises to answer it.

Shai Skymatsky looks forward to seeing his best friend, his dearest friend. He looks forward to meeting his American wife, Carolyn, and the American children. They are coming to sit shiva and pay their respects to a great sabra: Yakov Solomon.

In the little Toyota, Maya is completely silent. So quiet Shai wonders if she has fallen asleep. He wonders if she is angry at him for insisting she go. It will be good for you, he'd said. You will see all your old friends!

Maya stares out the window. Shai thinks of Marc with pleasure. How they were so young! With so much hair. Shai is bald.

Shai had once thought Marc had all the luck in the universe. He remembers how brown their skin was. How stoned they were those six months on the beaches of Thailand. The time they nearly drowned in their operation, how Marc got his gun stuck and would not cut it loose. How Shai stayed beside him and would not swim to the surface without his partner. And how good that made the life that came after. His wife is so quiet he can hardly hear her breathe. She must be sleeping. She is tired more and more as the pregnancy progresses. She sleeps so much Shai Skymatsky imagines she will give birth in her sleep. Her mouth hangs open sweetly, like a child. Her breath rattles wetly in her throat.

Tel Aviv gives way to the high-rises on the outskirts. To Shai Skymatsky, they look like the projects in America from the days he lived in New York. Shai loves so dearly his tiny apartment near the beach. The high-rise apartments look like ghettos, but they are expensive and all Israel wants to live in them. There are lengthy waiting lists.

Would you like to have one of those apartments, dear Mayush? Shai says to the sleeping figure of his wife. Her shaded face is turned away from him. Her thick black hair ropes around her neck and shoulders. We could put a bundle of children in one of those big apartments and they could go to good schools.

She turns and groans, shields her eyes with her hand from the afternoon glare of the sun. No, she says, as she always says. Our apartment is plenty for us. It always makes Shai happy to hear this. She wants what I want, he thinks.

They drive through Alonim in silence. Should I stop and get an espresso? Shai asks. Some hummus? But there is no answer. Maya sleeps again.

Marc Solomon walks around the kibbutz. He walks past the tennis courts, now overgrown with weeds. The soccer field where he was unsurpassed as a player. The best in the north. If not for Shayetet 13, he might have turned professional, played for Beitar Jerusalem, or gone to Europe even. The swimming pool reflects the full moon. It's 30 degrees. Too warm for the lightweight wool sweater Marc wears. It is three o'clock in the morning.

He's drunk from the whiskey he'd brought to the lul. Four bottles purchased duty-free. He'd hidden them away from his sister and the funeral, his mother and uncles. His friends are happy to see him, shy. Telling him the kibbutz gossip. The same gossip from twenty years ago. A long news cycle, in fact a loop. The marriages and betrayals. The crack-ups and suicide attempts. Yes, he knew about his ex-girlfriend Maya Frank. Yes, he'd heard she'd married his old army buddy and friend from the next kibbutz over, Shai Skymatsky.

Yes, it was funny what they said about Shai Skymatsky. The stories of the commandos. The operation by the sea and how'd he flagged down the entire army with a Sprite bottle and a flashlight. Shai was coming tomorrow and he was bringing Maya, of all people.

Someone drain the swimming pool! Maya Frank is coming! his friend Ofer had called out, and they'd laughed.

Ofer, you're such an asshole, Marc had said, and everyone groaned and it was time to go.

Marc has slept a couple of hours in his parents' basement apartment, but the peacocks' calls have woken him and now he is wandering, jet-lagged. Past the cowshed, past the wadi, past the orchards, the pecan trees, the pomegranates, the morning glories that climb the railings, closed up for the night. The water tower where some girl had jumped some years before. His sister Keren's house.

Carolyn will come tomorrow with the boys.

Guy Gever sits out on a porch chair surrounded by five sleeping hounds who barely raise their heads as Marc approaches. Gever! Marc says.

Solomon. Guy doesn't get up. He gestures for Marc to sit.

Well, we've been through the shit now, haven't we, Guy Gever says.

Yes, I guess we have.

Such a shame. There was a time when Marc Solomon could do no wrong.

And you, Guy Gever. You were king in this kibbutz for over thirty years. What have you been reduced to?

Guy laughs. He sucks at one end of a spliff and offers it to Marc. Why not? Marc takes it and sucks in the acrid marijuana mixed with tobacco. I did not know you smoked.

I don't, Guy says. This is a special occasion. He watches Marc inhale. Careful now, Guy says. This is strong stuff. From Sinai. Strong enough to stone even the Bedouin.

The moon is impossibly large in the sky. There are more stars here than there are in Los Angeles. The moment feels holy. Marc Solomon is not religious, but he can understand how the night and stars could be mistaken for *God*. Guy is humming an old Hasidic song they'd learned as children for their bar mitzvah. *All the world is a narrow bridge*, Guy Gever sings in his good high tenor voice, *do not be afraid*.

It doesn't take long for Marc to realize he is very, very high. Guy Gever begins talking. For a moment Marc sinks into it, the words. Guy is telling him things the rabbi has told him. The old rabbi who has been indoctrinating the kids as they return from their months in India, after the army, high on spirituality. It is some kind of mystical mumbo jumbo. Marc never gets high, but he is high now. Suddenly, the world has no seams. He doesn't believe in taking drugs of any kind. Even three years ago when he'd had his wisdom teeth removed it was his wife, Carolyn, who took all of his pain meds for recreation. He likes to drink. Like a man. Like his father. Marc pulls himself together, looks at Guy Gever with pity. For surely it is the kibbutz that has made him like this. If Guy Gever had gotten to the real world, even only as far away as Haifa, he would have been better off. He's grown soft here, that's what it is. It is not reality here in the kibbutz.

You, now! Guy shouts at him suddenly. You, Marc Solomon, imagine that if a man takes this step, all carefully considered, life will go as smoothly as a reserves exercise, is that it, Marc Solomon?

But Marc had not been speaking, not out loud anyway. Or had he? Maybe he was speaking. Marc is a rational man. But then Marc is sweating, profusely. His hands are clenched into fists. He wants to get up and leave, very much.

You could just run, you know, Guy says to Marc. You have enough money, don't you? I thought you and Ziv were in competition to see who would be the wealthiest Solomon? You could just run away and never come back and leave all your family and legal problems behind.

Like you did, Guy Gever? When you tried to run away to Jordan?

That was a long time ago, Guy says. And anyway, it was not for lack of trying. I didn't have the money to go anywhere. Nor proper visas. I'm afraid of flying and it is impossible to get out of this godforsaken country without a flight.

A boat to Cyprus, then.

Guy shrugs again. I hate boats. What can I tell you? I'm a man of the earth. I like the earth. I am afraid of everything that is not the earth, the bushes, and the trees.

Like my father, Marc says.

Yes, Guy says. Like your father. Everything that is not built on earth. On soil. I need roots. The earth Abraham walked on. Guy Gever takes a long pull and the homemade cigarette burns bright red in the night. For instance, now your father is as safe as a baby in his crib. He lies in the cement of his grave. Nothing more can happen to him.

Yes, well. You are safe, Guy. Nothing bad can happen to you here.

Something bad can always happen, Guy tells him. And it will.

Gever goes on and on, Here is a story your father told me years ago when Keren and I were first dating: Back in the old times, when he was small, there was a chief of a Druze village in the north named Kemal Kasem. Your grandfather used to like to tell stories about him. He was very strong in his village. Why was he strong in his village? your father asked. Because he had killed eleven men. Blood feud, you know. How did they know he killed eleven men? Yakov asked. Why not ten or a dozen? Because the neighbor counts. You see, Marc? Because the neighbor counts!

Yes, Marc has heard this one before. Marc begins to doze off. Guy says, She's coming for you. And if you see Maya, let her go. Let her drown herself. It's better. I hear she's coming back. I should have let her drown.

Oh, come on. Marc gets up to leave.

No, it's true. Let me tell you something, Marc Solomon. You either fuck her or let her drown. That's the best you can do. You should have married her. You never should have left. You were the one who should have stayed. If you'd stayed, you would have made the kibbutz good. But you went, and look what has happened. Guy spreads his arms wide. Look what has happened to all of us.

But you are doing well now! Marc says and laughs.

Guy laughs too and then is quiet. Yes, he says. In a way. But you are not.

An hour later, Marc is trudging home, head spinning, mostly from the tobacco that he is not used to. He wonders if Guy Gever said any of those things at all. He wonders if Guy was even there. Could it be he sat on that porch, as he had many times while on leave from the army, but this time by himself? Could he have made up Guy Gever? And if he *was* there, could they have just sat silently?

Maybe it's true. He never should have left the kibbutz.

Carolyn and the boys will arrive tomorrow so Sam Solomon could play in the regional soccer championship. Dror will pick them up and bring them to the kibbutz to sit shiva and visit the grave site.

Chapter 25

MARC IN THE KIBBUTZ

WHEN MARC first sees Maya, he notes she is fuller than her Facebook picture. On Facebook one sees middle-aged women falling into one of two categories. Since it is impossible for them to stay exactly as they were as teenagers, they either 1) become quite fat, or at least a little fat, or 2) become lean and sinewy. Hard and tough as leather shoelaces.

Maya is one of the exceptions to the rule. Her skin is shiny and youthful, with not a single line on her face. Only a barely discernible crease between the eyebrows. Her curly hair drapes luxuriously over her shoulders. Gone are her dreadlocks. Her breasts spill out of her V-neck T-shirt. She had always been flat-chested. He remembers how she was one of the only girls in the kibbutz who could get away with not wearing a bra. She is still not wearing a bra and her nipples are pronounced, standing high beneath her shirt.

She is a vision.

Shyly, he approaches her. She wraps her arms around his neck and kisses his cheek. Marc feels his face grow hot. He has always blushed. He blushes now. And standing off to the side is his old friend, Shai Skymatsky.

Hello! Hello! Shai says. He embraces Marc. He squeezes him so tightly Marc loses his breath. For the first time since he landed, Marc exhales.

Can we walk with you? Shai asks. Maya has retreated a few steps away.

Come back, Marc thinks.

Marc has a theory that no one loves anyone after a certain age. We are, none of us, really capable of it. Right about the time you stop enjoying discovering new music, that's the moment you are incapable of love. Everything beyond that moment is as mechanical as a wind-up toy. It is all memory and ghosts. And yet.

Marc thinks of his father, his voice booming. He is telling a story, a joke. The hair from a woman down there can derail a train! he says. No really! Yakov says. Think about it.

I'm only going to the kol-bo to pick up a few things for my mother and for Keren, Marc says.

How is Vivienne? Maya asks.

She is all right, I guess. Maybe even better off.

And man! How are you? Shai asks. He's bounding around with his enormous energy like a big, happy dog. Marc notes he's a little fat now. Solomon! How are you faring these days?

Marc stops. Are you talking about my case?

Yes, of course. What else?

Marc stops walking. He's still wearing the suit pants he wore on the flight the day before and an old T-shirt of Yakov's.

Carolyn's flight is due to arrive in Tel Aviv any moment. The dust kicked up by their walking settles. Marc bends over and dusts himself off with the palms of his hands. Maya's feet in her sandals are brown, her toes are a little dirty and unpedicured. Carolyn would never walk around with her feet like that. Maya's ankles are small and delicate. Marc heard she'd married Shai Skymatsky, of course, but he never expected she'd be radiant. She stands like a goddess in her cut-off jeans. Shai sees Marc staring and pulls Maya closer to him. Yes, Shai is proud of his trophy. Why shouldn't he be? He caught what everyone else had thrown back into the sea.

Well, Marc says. I'm fine. Everything is fine. It was all blown out of proportion. I was never even charged with a crime! It is an American custom. The police accuse you of a crime and then take all your money. But it is not serious, Marc says. Everything is in civil courts now.

Oh, fantastic! Shai says. Of course I knew everything was all right.

Marc catches Maya's eye. Maya turns away. Once, when they were teenagers, how well they knew each other. His roommate was a deep sleeper. Marc was responsible for waking him each morning, always waiting until just after Maya had sneaked back to her own room. As the first light fell into their dorm room, he would wake up with Maya astride him—

It's good to see you, Marc, Maya says now. She's holding Shai's arm. Shai seems to be nuzzling her ear. Marc looks away. His heart pounds a strange rhythm. We'll be staying at my mom's. Come have coffee with us later.

They take off down the path and Marc heads toward the kol-bo, the general store. When Marc was growing up, this was the place where the children picked up their one chocolate bar a week and where the mothers shopped for small items for the home. At one point, most meals were taken in the dining hall. There was only a small store, no supermarkets as there were now, since the dining rooms of the kibbutzim had closed. The kol-bo was now like a New York City bodega. Only the old women who didn't drive shopped there still. The younger families drove into town to the big American-style supermarkets.

Marc Solomon! It is Mrs. Benjamin. She is English and awkward and hasn't learned Hebrew after forty years in the kibbutz. She has always liked the Solomons, who, for the most part, all speak good English. Your father was a wonderful man, she says to Marc, who is now pressed against Mrs. Benjamin's breasts. He feels a slight tingle. That strange attraction the male has to the maternal. Her own husband dead now less than a year.

He always made the ladies feel special, your father. You always felt like you were special when your father was talking to you.

I'll bet you did, Marc thinks.

Thank you, Mrs. Benjamin, Marc says. How have you been?

She grabs hold of his arm with wizened hands. Blue veins pop, and Marc almost flinches to see them. Her breath is minty. The rumor is she's not Jewish and never converted. They say she was Mar Benjamin's wartime English bride. She leans in. To tell you the truth, I've never been happier since my husband, that old bastard, is gone! My goodness, she says. I feel like a young girl again.

Marc is speechless. Mrs. Benjamin steps away, watching his face, and then chuckles as she pushes her tiny shopping cart down the narrow aisle of the kol-bo.

Yes, as a matter of fact Marc can imagine his father and Mrs. Benjamin. When she'd laughed just then, he'd seen her beauty. Marc was not like his father, had never been like his father, had done everything in his power to be nothing like his father. It had not occurred to him how much the women might want it.

Marc closes his eyes and sees Carolyn in Dror's car, hurtling across Israel, a land she doesn't care for, on her way to him.

Chapter 26

GABRIEL

GABRIEL SAT on the floor and played Joseph's mother's CDs. He leaned up against his army-green duffle bag. Joseph lay on the couch and felt his eyes grow heavy. The clock on the stereo said it was 1:30 a.m. But Joseph's belly was full and Gabriel was nice. Like a real brother. Like family.

Gabriel was also tired. His frame sprawled out across the thin rug. His bones dug into the wood floor, but he was too weary to get up. And he also didn't want to startle Joseph, who looked like he was about to fall asleep. Gabriel knew that on the table by the front door of the apartment there was a set of keys, and Joseph's grandfather's credit card.

In California, I play soccer. Do you play soccer, Joseph?

Joseph nodded his head. Yes, he said. Of course. I am the best in my grade. I am going to be a professional and play for Beitar Jerusalem. His head fell onto the sofa cushion. He'd fallen asleep.

Gabriel waited several moments and then crept across the room toward the table beside the door. The floorboards creaked.

Joseph stirred but didn't waken. Gabriel stood very still. The card glinted in the light of a street lamp just outside the living room window. He exhaled in his new freedom. The apartment and the boy's act of sleep had finally released him from scrutiny.

His conscience pained him. Certainly the boy owed him nothing, even if he was Gabriel's brother. The boy's mother owed him nothing, nor did the grandfather. But still. He was a stranger in a strange land. Even if it was the land of his birth, the birth of haaretz had been an accident. He realized now, and finally without pain, that he was the least Israeli of his brothers and cousins. He'd spent the bulk of his childhood in America. He'd even had his bar mitzvah in Los Angeles. His mother had left religion behind when they'd left Jerusalem. Three years in the IDF was not going to change anything.

No, he did not want to go to the West Bank. No, he did not want to go to the Golani. No, he did not want to protect settlers. No, he did not want to sit at a desk and be an administrator for a bunch of fascist soldiers.

No, he did not want to go to military prison.

This occupation. How had he not known these things when he was back in the United States? He had known but not fully understood.

His hand hovered over the credit card. Joseph spoke, slurring his words, still asleep. Gabriel snatched his hand away. Now was not the time. He needed a shower. He'd caught a glimpse of it, its walls covered in stone. There was a large rainfall showerhead that he looked forward to standing under. Showers in the army had been limited. There had been all those other soldiers, and the *incident*.

Gabriel shucks off his uniform, leaving it in a heap on the floor of the bathroom. On second thought, he shoved it into the hamper. He would like never to see it again. He'd leave it for the boy as a souvenir of his visit. The normalcy of a hamper full of dirty clothing brought tears to his eyes. He thought of his mother, back home. He was not certain he would be welcome, only that he must get there by any means necessary.

The shower was hot and rinsed the army down the drain. He pissed too. The smell was fragrant in the steam. There was expensive American shampoo and he washed his buzzed head twice. He shaved his face and neck with Joseph's mother's razor. He used conditioner as shaving cream. He thought of Joseph's mother. He saw her in a movie years ago with his brothers. She was a little full now, photographs around the apartment showed, but she only looked more beautiful. Not like the starved American actresses back in LA. He did not think of his father. In fact, he rarely if ever thought of his father. He took himself in hand and when he came, minutes later, he sprayed the wall of the shower. After he stepped out and dried himself, he dressed in jeans and a T-shirt from his duffle bag.

He stepped into the living room, where the boy was still sleeping, only now there was a cat perched on the boy's back. The cat eyed him as he crossed the room. The boy didn't move. The cat stretched out and rested its chin on the boy's back. Its eyes flashed yellow.

I'll book the cheapest flight, Gabriel told himself. In his six months of service, he had made only five hundred shekels a month: about one hundred fifty dollars. In Joseph's room, he found the computer. No password, luckily. He pressed the space bar and the screen lit up. He typed in "Ben Gurion to JFK." Maybe he didn't need to go back to California, after all. He knew someone in New York City, a friend of his older brother who Gabriel had heard was doing quite well. His name was Tomer Skymatsky. He had a job on Wall Street.

There were a multitude of things he could do! He could go to college! Play soccer! No, the army was not for him.

Haaretz was not for him.

He would return his Israeli passport to the consulate the moment he got back to the States and he would never come back to this place—not knowing, of course, that he would not be let out. That he would be forced to return to the army until they proved his incompetency to serve, and released him back to America.

Chapter 27

Dror Solomon

CAROLYN IS so exhausted after the flight, she nearly forgets Nicholas on the airplane. He is inconsolable, sleepy and miserable from the long flight. Izaac is dragging him by the hand through customs. They show their passports. Izaac and Sam both have Israeli passports, though Izaac insists he'll give his up in another year or so to avoid the draft. Of course he will, Marc had said. We are American now. It is the reasonable thing to do. But the official won't leave it alone. You must get a passport for the youngest as well, the official says.

Izaac rolls his eyes. He can have mine.

Izaac! Carolyn hisses. She's had trouble with Israeli customs before. She's been escorted off planes and strip-searched. Until she understood, and memorized a Hebrew name, the name of her rabbi, the name of her synagogue. This was de rigueur each and every time she'd flown. It didn't help that she was semi-fluent in Hebrew, though she'd thought it might. It was only a red flag. A suspicious activity by an American non-Jew.

As they walk through the door to the cavernous room of luggage carousels a woman grabs her arm and speaks to her in Russian. I'm sorry, Carolyn says. I don't understand. She tries again in Hebrew, Slicha, ani lo mevina.

Izaac smirks at her. She thinks you're Russian. He points to her yoga pants. They appear to be covered in dog hair. Those look communist-issued, he says. You look like shit, Mom.

Carolyn is stunned almost to tears, tries to rub the dog hair off. Puberty makes children mean, Carolyn thinks.

At the baggage carousel they grab their luggage. Carolyn tries to activate her cell phone but it doesn't work. Marc must have forgotten to set up the international account.

They find Dror Solomon waiting for them outside the airport.

Dror pulls over to the side, curses the policeman who tries to wave him on. He grabs their suitcases, ruffles Izaac's hair, and asks how their flight was. The children load sleepily into the backseat of the car and Carolyn climbs into the passenger seat.

So, you know all about Tomer Skymatsky? Dror Solomon says. Shame, isn't it. Little brother of Shai Skymatsky. You ever hear what they say about him?

Carolyn flinches, recoils. No, she says. I don't really feel like talking about it. It was a long flight—

Wonder why he did it.

I don't know the details, she says. She pinches the tense skin between her eyebrows.

You think Marc knew anything about it? I mean, the firm was doing really well, I hear. For sure, he did! The whole database of Tomer's gambling operation was on Marc's server! All the money he was pretending to bring in from the religious was really *bets*. He was a common bookie!

I beg your pardon?

Listen to me, Dror says. He grips the wheel tightly. He is going only forty miles per hour. Tel Aviv traffic races around him. Carolyn suspects the children will fall asleep. I've been hearing rumors for *months*. Tomer was a bookie. You know. Sports bets. Police don't like that much. Marc is lucky Tomer wasn't taking money from Israel or this would be a much more serious matter.

I don't know, Carolyn says, and closes her eyes. She clenches her fists tight in her lap. Carolyn Bennett Solomon is *furious*. The words she'd like to say sizzle and dissolve in her mouth as if on hot coals. Angry to be stuck with Dror Solomon. A man she despises and who despises her back, it would appear. The Solomon brothers can hardly tolerate each other ever since a real estate partnership turned ugly a year ago. Marc had put money into a discotheque Dror was developing in Tel Aviv, but something had gone wrong. The money had disappeared.

But Carolyn can't afford to rent a car. So she's stuck. Dror comes because he's closest to Ben Gurion and saves Marc a four-hour round trip. Carolyn knows she should be grateful. She grips the door handle of the car with two hands. Dror drives his father's car, of course. Already the spoils are divided.

No, I *do* know, he tells her, in that typical aggro way of a certain kind of Israeli. "Aggro." A word Izaac would use. *Don't be so aggro, bro.* She glances over at Dror now. His jaw tense and working. His arms are sinewy. Clearly he's lost weight since marrying this second wife. He's been going to the gym. She wonders if he's taking steroids. It seems unusual that a man in his late forties should be so cut. It is an American thought. Israelis don't consume pharmaceuticals the way Americans do. A little coke. A blunt. They drink, but not much.

I mean, he continues, aren't you *nervous?* Did you see what they wrote about him? It was all over the news here!

Carolyn turns around in her seat. All three children are sound asleep. Thank God.

Don't get me wrong! I love my brother. But I'm worried about him. I'm worried about you and the kids. The police will come for you too, you know, just like they did for Bernie Badoff—

Madoff.

Whatever. And your children! What will you do to protect them? Their *reputation?*

Shut up, Dror.

I'm sorry?

Shut up. Just shut the fuck up. Be quiet already. The kids are in the back of the car for God's sake.

Oh, I see. Dror speeds up. The car veers nearly to the shoulder. You know, it wasn't easy coming to get you at the airport. Your flight was two hours early. The traffic was terrible.

Carolyn is getting a migraine. The traffic is terrible now. It's Thursday night; everyone is heading out of the city. They slow to a crawl. Dror tells her it will be another hour at least. Possibly two!

Everything Dror says seems calculated for maximum damage. Especially anything he says with a smile. Carolyn smiles weakly back. The children sleep.

Carolyn reaches into her bag at her feet. Her body hurts. The migraine pulses, marching up the side of her skull. Her mouth is dry from the airplane, dry from the air outside. But she's freezing. Dror has the air-conditioning turned up high. She fishes through the pockets of her bag. Her hand wades through half-wrapped tampons, an open pack of gum, a bottle of water that has emptied itself into the bottom of her bag, her now damp wallet, her wet passport and the soggy passports of her three boys. Finally she finds the little plastic box where she keeps her earplugs. She opens the box and fishes out a quarter of a Valium and an Ambien. She works up some saliva in her mouth and swallows the pills. Dror watches her, intently. Too intently for a man who is driving with his knees.

Please, Dror, Carolyn says. Please just drive. I'm sorry. I'm just tired. . . . It was a long flight.

Okay! You want to stop and get a coffee? We can stop in Alonim. They have good espresso.

She should. She needs to pee . . . but to wake up the boys? To prolong this trip another minute longer? Before she can answer, Dror pulls off the highway into a small shopping center. The children wake up, complaining. Nicholas begins crying immediately. Dror winces. He opens the door and pulls the crying child out by his arm. Be strong now, little man, Dror says. Dror picks him up and carries him into the small shopping center.

Sam stumbles out of the car after the oldest. Izaac's eyes are narrowed into angry slits. He's already clamped his headphones over his ears. Carolyn knows he knows what's going on, but she can't seem to say anything to him about it. Sam holds Carolyn's hand. He is the sweetest of the three boys, the most innocent. More innocent even than his little brother. Mommy, Sam says, why does Dror say we need to be protected?

Mmmhmm, Carolyn says, and thinks: Maybe, just maybe, the children don't need to be protected. Maybe they *shouldn't* be protected.

Carolyn bends down and whispers in his ear, Never mind, darling. He's talking nonsense.

He's talking shtuyot? Sam asks.

Yes, she says, and she smiles. Such a smart boy. Shtuyot, indeed.

Children survive so much worse, Carolyn thinks.

The children order pastries. Carolyn orders a café hafuch, Two shots, please. She's regretting taking the Valium and the Ambien. It spreads through her body, slowly poisoning her. Always this: first the burning and then the peace. Her little one has left his uncle and comes to her. The middle child holds onto her other arm. In twenty minutes, God willing, she'll be okay. Sleeping pills are like a big wave. You can let it knock you down and drag you under or you can ride it out. If you ride it out, it will not knock you down. The coffee helps. As much as Israel is hard, the coffee and food are delicious. The first time she ever smelled a cucumber was in Israel. Dror orders sandwiches for them both. He folds his arms high on his chest, like Yakov would have, and waits. After a moment more, it registers with

Carolyn that she must pay. She has money from an old account she'd kept in her maiden name, from her first job in the city. She pulls out a debit card. This money was meant for emergencies.

Wasn't that the real injustice in this world? To have more than one needed?

She can hardly look at Dror now, she is so full of contempt. For the way he told his parents about Marc's situation. Carolyn had heard how he'd burst in with his terrible smile. *What?* he'd said to Yakov and Vivienne, *you sit so calm and comfortable? Haven't you seen the news? Haven't you read the newspaper? Your son sits in jail! His company in shambles! His bank accounts cleared out!*

She can just imagine it.

Vivienne had called Carolyn, crying and panicked. So panicked she'd started hyperventilating. Vivienne, Vivienne, Carolyn had said. It's okay. He's okay. The lawyers will sort through everything. Al tidagi. Al tidagi. Don't worry.

But did he do it?

Back in the car, Dror thinks he's whispering. I met with Tomer Skymatsky, just before it happened. He wanted in on a real estate deal he'd heard I was doing. He came to Israel, for Pesach. Did you know? Then I heard later from Moti, an old friend of Tomer's, that Tomer was running a gambling ring through Marc's firm! Moti told me Tomer had fifty thousand dollars wrapped in tinfoil in his suitcase. Tomer was so nervous he accidentally checked his bags. He figured he'd be better off if the money was stolen by baggage handlers. He was really afraid of getting caught. Tomer's been running money through the datiyim and through the firm for years. I think that fifty grand was his retirement money, or seed money for a new venture. Moti said Tomer's in Eilat now.

None of this is true, Carolyn says, shaking her head.

What? You didn't know? You think Marc didn't know? Come on. Don't be naïve! But don't worry . . . I never told Yakov anything about what I know.

But you did.

He looks at her. Come on. You mad about that too? They deserved to know! Nathalie thought it was a good idea. What if Marc needed help or money?

Carolyn brings her hands to her temples. The Ambien has loosened its grip on her.

Marc would never take money from Yakov, she says. Nor would I.

Yeah, Dror snorts. I'll bet.

Dror curses the traffic and Carolyn dozes with her head against the warm glass of the window.

Chapter 28

Marc and Maya by the Cypress Trees

T HEY USED to meet in the fields behind the row of cypress trees. Marc would bring an apple. When he came home on leave from the navy, they'd spend a few hours in the fields. They'd put down a quilt and make coffee on a small camping stove and smoke cigarettes. The apple would be warm from Marc's cargo shorts pocket. Maya would kiss him chastely on the cheek and Marc would grab her and shove his tongue down her throat. He wasn't subtle, Marc, at sixteen, and he wasn't even the best lover she'd had. But Maya loved him. She was crazy for him. They used to meet after Shabbat dinner. She would bring the quilt from her bed and they would lie down on it.

The moon is full and Maya is taking a walk. She feels her old depression returning. Shai Skymatsky is one kibbutz over, drinking with his brothers. She'd begged off. She's tired. The pregnancy and all. Truth is, she hasn't been able to eat anything in days. The morning sickness has started. She thought she'd escaped it—she's already in her sixteenth week. She's not showing yet, except for a small belly.

She's brought with her that same quilt she had as a teenager. The one she used to lie on with Marc Solomon. The smell of it pains her. She'd like to shove it in her mouth and eat it. She'd found the blanket in a closet underneath all the old mopping towels. She'd stuffed it into her fabric bag along with a bottle of beer. What's one bottle of beer to a fetus the size of a fig? She pulls an apple from a tree. It is small, hard, and bitter.

She never imagined he'd be there, but there he is. Marc Solomon. Smoking a cigarette. He was one of the only boys who didn't smoke in high school and didn't take it up in the army. All his recent troubles. She wants to tell him to stop smoking, as though he still belongs to her. Her husband smokes, but he does it furtively because it bothers her. Ever since she got pregnant, seeing him smoke makes her more and more upset. Now Shai does it just before he jumps into the sea every evening at sunset. He throws the butt into the sand, then dives into the sea to wash the smell away. He swims far out from the shore, and this, too, worries Maya—that one day he will swim so far, he won't make it back. Everything worries Maya these days. But at the same time, tentatively, almost secretively, she is happy and hopeful.

Marc Solomon has always smelled sweet, like he sweats sugar water. He sees her. She draws up beside him and gives him a small, furtive hug. Hello, he says, and hugs her back. Her parents hadn't liked Marc. And Vivienne and Yakov had not liked Maya. There had never even been a goodbye. It was so long ago. She couldn't quite remember everything. Only recently, she'd found him on Facebook and friended him. She'd spent a few minutes flipping through the posts, mostly his American wife's. What a perfect life they had. Three perfect children. More American than Israeli. Then Shai had told her about Marc's troubles. It seemed Shai's brother had somehow been involved, although Shai refused to believe it. No one knew exactly how, and no one had spoken to Tomer Skymatsky in two years, not since he'd borrowed all that money from Shai and their mother for a real estate deal. Ganav ben ganav, they'd said about Tomer, arguably the smartest of the Skymatsky children. Thief, son of a thief. Too smart. For his father had also done bad things, and had run away to South Africa and was never seen again.

Maya and Marc say nothing. Peacocks cry out from the Valley. Maya wants to ask Marc if he's done it, the thing, whatever it is, he's been accused of back in the States. Gambling, was it? She feels certain, somehow, that he will tell her. And Marc wants to tell her how great she looks. How it's impossible that after twenty years she looks exactly the same. Even her hairstyle hasn't changed. Just past her shoulders, the same dark brown, the same wavy texture. Could it be that no time has passed?

Marc glances at her shoulder; her shirt hangs off it and he can see that the skin on her chest and neck is smooth and brown. He wants to reach out and touch her. She wants to ask him her questions but she doesn't dare. The clouds part and the stars shine. The moon is near full and Marc clears his throat and says, I didn't do it. He says, I didn't know anything about it. I didn't know Shai's little brother was a fucking *bookie*. Marc runs his hand through his hair. His still glorious hair. He's haggard, sure, and older too, but he's the same Marc. The same irrepressible kid who went into the army and got his ass kicked but won in the end, and went to America and got his ass kicked but won in the end, and then lost everything. He's changed too. He's broken and trembling and he reaches out to Maya and takes her hand, and Maya sees she hasn't changed at all. She still wants what she's not supposed to have. The bottomless wanting is what will ruin her in the end because bottomless wanting is like falling through a well. Everything one desires is a tenuous little shelf that only briefly breaks the fall. So Marc reaches for Maya and Maya reaches for Marc. She could love him. She closes her eyes in dread. How will she face Shai again? How will she ever look him in the eye? Marc is moving closer to her, he is slipping his arm around her waist.

But the beer is not sitting well in her stomach. Not at all. First comes the sweating. Then her stomach heaves. An odd croaking sound arises from her throat and Marc backs away, confused. The apple, saliva, and beer all shoot out of her mouth and onto the ground. There are flecks of vomit on Marc's shoe. What the fuck? Marc says in English, and steps away. Infidelity should be clean. It should be easy. There shouldn't be a single glitch that causes either party to say, Let's call the whole thing off.

Marc turns and walks quickly away from Maya. Marc, who has never cheated on his wife, convinces himself nothing happened. Nothing happened. Nothing was going to happen. Nothing will ever happen. He walks quickly through the kibbutz, barely registering his surroundings, until he is running. His heart is bursting. Carolyn is waiting for him on the couch. I just woke up, she tells him. And she smiles.

Chapter 29

AND SHIRA

SHIRA, IN a fit of pique, has married her old boyfriend, the Buddhist, Asaf Boulboulim. Asaf Boulboulim, who'd once vowed never to marry. Michael, her boyfriend in Los Angeles, is furious. When she returns to LA, she will break up with Michael. Or perhaps when she sees Michael, she will want to break up with Asaf. Shira is tired of going back and forth to Los Angeles. Joseph is growing up. He won't be in the house much longer. Already, since his bar mitzvah he seems to have less and less use for her.

It is a religious ceremony. The rabbi is Asaf's family rabbi. He is a new Russian immigrant and claims to be the descendant of a great rabbi in Kiev, but no one believes him. People question if he is even really Jewish. They say the rabbi's wedding pictures were taken in a cathedral.

Her sister, Keren, is a surprising ally. She comes with Guy Gever, who wears a kippa on his head. The women wear white. Joseph refuses to come. He has a girlfriend now and spends all his time at her house, near the Old City. He lives with his father now.

Shira is starring in a feature film with a wide release. An *American* film. Sean Penn is producing. She goes to Cannes on her own merit this year. And Sundance, and Venice too. Shira is ecstatically happy.

She doesn't need Michael anymore. She has her own money. She invests forty thousand shekels in a vaping bar. It opens down the street from her apartment. She spends another twenty thousand shekels redoing her apartment. She gives up, for now, her dream of moving to Tel Aviv.

But Shira has just met a man of indeterminate age. He wears the hipster uniform of skintight pants that bag fetchingly around his crotch area and those Havaianas flip-flops that are so popular now. His sunglasses are real Ray-Bans, not knockoffs. Ray-Bans that in Israel can cost as much as one thousand shekels. But of course he bought them in New York. Yes, and he knows her brother too. Don't tell Marc you know me, he tells her. We had an argument back in the States. He is looking for a place to stay and a bank account to hold his money.

Her new boyfriend fucks her in what was recently Asaf Boulboulim's office. The lovers have taken all Asaf's things—the saffron robes and sandalwood beads—and thrown them into boxes, which they placed on the street beside the cats and other garbage. He takes care to change the locks, and he does it himself—another skill he'd picked up in New York, where all the locksmiths are Israeli. Asaf pounds on the door while Shira is on her hands and knees on the living room floor and Tomer Skymatsky rocks behind her.

Tomer, Shira shouts, again and again. Tomer! Tomer!

Chapter 30

VIVIENNE

VIVIENNE GETS used to Yakov's passing. People speak more freely now about Yakov. She knows about his affairs. She knows now about Maya and the beautiful baby Maya has called Yakov. She thinks tenderly of Maya. Every once in a while, at the kol-bo, she sees Maya's mother. There is no point in avoiding her. Vivienne has never liked her, has never had a conversation with her in her life. What could Yakov have ever seen in her? Maya's mother. She must have been thrilled Yakov was interested in her. It was like an act of charity.

Once, Vivienne was the most beautiful woman in the kibbutz. It is only natural she should have competitors. It is only natural that women should want to topple her off the pedestal where once she reigned. Including Maya's appallingly plain mother. A woman who let her daughter attempt suicide again and again until finally the kibbutz doctor had Maya committed. It was almost as though Maya's mother, whose name Vivienne refused to say out loud, or even in her head, wanted to wipe Maya away like a stain. And such a lovely girl was Maya. Really, one of the loveliest girls in the kibbutz. Judging from the old photographs in the kibbutz archives, she took after Yakov's mother, who'd died so young.

What a shame it was that Yakov had never seen his baby grandson, the tiny Yakov Skymatsky. And a shame that tiny Yakov Skymatsky had no father. His father drowned foolishly swimming one kilometer out to sea. Taken by a strong undercurrent, it was said. In the kibbutz they laughed and said Shai Skymatsky had run away, no doubt. Probably had swum out to Cyprus and was living out some island dream far away from responsibility, from fatherhood, from the reserves. But of course they only joked that way because of their heartbreak.

Meanwhile, Dror was in a fury trying to substantiate the rumors that money had gone to Maya's child. They'd each received their share. Even Ziv. It wasn't as much as they'd hoped. Had Maya received more? Ziv had not even bothered to come to the funeral, though deep down who could blame him? Dror had threatened to spend every shekel of his own money trying to get that money back. Had there been a DNA test? There should be a DNA test! Until then, Maya shouldn't get anything.

But don't be silly, Dror! Vivienne had said. Look at how much money you have. Don't be so greedy. Let it go, already! And she has lost her *husband!*

With her money, Vivienne will take her friend Aliza to Prague. She's always wanted to go. She and Aliza will travel first class. And she'll buy herself a new Louis Vuitton bag from the fancy mall in Jerusalem. And maybe, if she has the energy, she'll move away from this kibbutz. Move to Jerusalem where her sister lives, close to Shira and Joseph, or Tel Aviv. Maybe Los Angeles.

Or Paris.

She'd like to visit Ziv in Singapore.

Vivienne goes to the kitchen and pours herself a glass of water. There is a pair of Yakov's spectacles at the far end of the countertop. Vivienne picks them up between two fingers and deposits them in the trash. She feels sprightly. She feels like dancing. She feels like the fifteen-year-old who left Algiers for the new country. She raises her glass and toasts the air.

L'JahHanim! she says.

To hell with them!

Chapter 31

GEVER

THEY LOOKED good. Guy Gever was very fit. He'd let his hair grow out from his usual army-style cut. It suited him. Marc's hair was thinning, and he had lost weight too. Marc had taken up running at the advice of his doctors. He had traveled to all the major cities to run marathons. Next month, he would be in Boston.

Guy Gever stood at his stove molding the ktsitsot, the meatballs he'd made from game his brothers shot the night before.

He turned to Marc Solomon. Still warm, he said, and laughed.

You look good, Guy, Marc said.

Yes, I do!

He'd recently made a mint. The paintball facility was a success. He paid a nominal fee to the kibbutz and the rest he kept for himself. But do you know who really looks good? Guy asked.

Nu? Marc said.

Your mother.

Yes? I was surprised she wasn't here. She hadn't even told me she was going to France. And she knew I was visiting, of course.

Just wait and you will really be surprised. What she tells you is not the whole truth. Only I know the truth. Yes. Your mother and I are good friends since Yakov died. Of course, I have always loved her. She supported me when no one else believed in me! And when Yakov died, I supported her emotionally. And yes, she is in France, but she is not with her sister. And she has money now. More than you can imagine. As you know, your father did not leave anyone very much. But guess where she is now?

Okay, Guy. So spill it. What is she doing?

Ha! Let me tell you! Did she ever tell you about a boyfriend she had in Algeria before she came to haaretz?

No, Marc said. He felt uneasy and shifted in his chair. He was also tired, jet-lagged from the journey. Keren came in through the sliding door and kissed him on both cheeks. She walked to Guy and embraced him. They stood there for a long moment. They had always been affectionate. Marc felt even more uncomfortable.

I'm going to take a shower, Keren said. Are you staying for dinner, motek?

Yes, he said. Of course.

Tov. Give me a minute to wash up.

Once Keren left, Guy poured two shots of vodka and brought them over to the sofas. Marc followed him there and settled into the deep cushions. I'll tell you fast, Guy said. Before Keren comes out. It's already very controversial, your mother. Everyone is very aggravated. But she just wants to be happy. You want her to be happy too, yes?

Betach. Of course I do.

Okay, shema. Listen: When she was a young girl, fourteen or fifteen, she fell hard for a boy named Antoine. He was Belgian, actually. His family was very wealthy. I think she told me they imported wine. He was not Jewish. They went to the same French school in Algiers. They fell madly in love. Of course, the relationship was doomed. Antoine's parents couldn't let him love a Jew and Vivienne's parents couldn't let her love a Catholic. And then she left for Israel. Antoine came not long after. He was a wrestler, a very good one. He came to Israel and he converted! Yes, the whole thing. Orthodox conversion. Lived with a religious family for six months and learned Hebrew. He even competed for Israel in the Olympics. But it wasn't enough. Your grandfather said no. Antoine wasn't really Jewish; he would never really be Jewish.

Okay, Marc said, downing his vodka. Go on.

So of course your grandfather kiboshed any chance of an engagement, though they were very deeply in love. Vivienne was already supposed to marry Yakov. She was at school in Jerusalem for a business degree when Antoine showed up. When Antoine saw that Vivienne would not marry him, he left Israel and he didn't return. He moved to Lyon and married. He had two or three children. And then, his wife died.

He decided to see what had happened to Vivienne Sarfati and about a year after he'd buried his wife, he returned to Israel to find her. He knew nothing about her. Didn't even know what her married name was. He had an old photograph and he carried it around Tel Aviv asking if anyone knew her.

Why Tel Aviv?

Guy shrugged. He never imagined Vivienne would stay in the kibbutz. He didn't imagine she was the kind of woman who would live in a kibbutz. She'd always loved the sea!

Okay, so——?

So, he ran into *Aliza*—they'd all been in the same school in Algiers—who was visiting her daughter who lives in Ramat Aviv. Israel is so small, you know, not like America. She recognized the picture and told Antoine that your mother was still on the kibbutz in the Jordan Valley. So one day, he showed up here. He had flowers. He had heard Yakov was dead and he was coming to find her.

And?

At that moment, Keren walked in.

Guy straightened up, arched his back and sat taller.

So she is there now? In Lyon? Marc asked. I thought she was traveling with her sister!

Oh, nu! Keren called from the kitchen. You swore you wouldn't tell anyone!

Hush, woman! He's bound to know sooner or later and, unlike the rest of you, he doesn't care! Guy leaned close to Marc and whispered, She is. She's there with him right now. And Antoine, he's a very wealthy man. And lastly: *Ziv* is with them! They are traveling with Ziv's husband, who owns a restaurant now in Yaffo. Don't worry. She'll be back in three days. You will have plenty of time to see her.

Marc walked to his mother's apartment along the dusty kibbutz path. Blue morning glories bloomed, wrapped tightly around the iron railing. Clothing hung on the neighbor's line. The birds chattered in the trees. A wind blew and scattered seeds and leaves and pollen across the path and into his hair.

Yom asal, yom basal, Marc thought. He'd thought this often recently. One day honey, the next day onions. It was an Arabic expression he'd heard from his father as a child, or perhaps it was from his saba Shimon. Or perhaps it had been imprinted in his DNA, long ago, before he was born.

Marc remembered his father laughing his big laugh, stroking his whiskers. His leg bobbing spasmodically over his knee. The men gathering around him, sipping coffee, sipping whiskey.

What to do about the Solomons? The Solomons will do for themselves.

Glossary of Hebrew Words

Kibbutz—communal living communities in Israel
Dorban—porcupine
Kinneret—Sea of Galilee
Lo gamur—not finished
Ima—mother
Shavuot—harvest holiday in spring
Tzimmer—similar to a bed and breakfast
Cartiv—popcicle
Lech mi po—get out of here
Shekels—Israeli money
Cushim—Africans
Bubbes—(Yiddish) grandmothers
Savtot—grandmothers
Marie de grêle—(French) Hail Mary prayer
Imaleh—mommy
Dod—uncle
Shayetet 13—Israeli navy commandos

Beitar Jerusalem—soccer team in Jerusalem

Saba—grandfather

Moshava—town; fashionable section within Jerusalem

Pitot—pita bread

Falafelim—falafel

Ktsitsot ve burekasim—meatballs and barakas, savory Bulgarian pastry

Savta—grandmother

Schnitzel—breaded, fried chicken cutlet

Balata—tile

Shoah—Holocaust

Ma kara—what happened?

Hadshote etmol—old news

Haaretz—newspaper or haaretz, the land (referring to Israel)

Glidot—ice creams

Cusit—hot girl

Zayin—prick (penis)

Baitsim—eggs

Nu—so?

Kippa—yarmulka

Tzitzit—religious article worn

Ha'mefaked—the commander

Lo—no

Slicha—excuse me

Kanyon—shopping mall

Baruch Hashem—God's blessing

Tachtonim—underwear

Metapelet—preschool caregiver

Lul—chicken house

Tachat—rear end/buttocks

Tzitzim—breasts

Ganon—preschool

Lecho—a kind of spicy tomato stew

Abba—father

Rav aluf—head of the army

Shtok—shut up!

Sukkot—fall jewish holiday

L'JahHanim—(Arabic) to hell with it

Menucha—rest or break

Achshav—now

Aravi—an Arabic person

Haverim—friends

Ma—what?

Yedioth ahronot—Israeli newspaper

Cheder ochel—dining room

Pilules—pills

Shiva—seven day rites after death

Kol-bo—the "all there" small kibbutz store

Betach—of course

Shema—listen

Yom asal, yom basal—(Arabic) one day honey, one day onion

Acknowledgments

Much gratitude and love to my agent, Duvall Osteen, and to Katie Raissian and Elisabeth Schmitz and the entire Grove team.

Deepest thanks to my friends and readers, especially Scott Wolven, Tim Dyke, Shanna McNair, Ophira Edut, Anna Shalom, David Hollander, Abi Keene, Steven Wagner, and Erin Lyons.

Love to my father, Robert Ball, for asking me to think deeply about the written and spoken word.

In loving memory of my mother, Clara Ball, and my teacher Jerry Brewster.

Most important, this book would not be possible without the sustained support and love of my husband. Good times and bad.

I'd also like to acknowledge the following sources: the documentary, *Children of the Sun* directed by Ran Tal and the essay entitled, "Like All Other Nations," by Grace Paley with respect to the line: "Who says we have to continue."

GROVE PRESS

Reading Group Guide

by Keturah Jenkins

WHAT TO DO ABOUT THE SOLOMONS

Bethany Ball

ABOUT THIS GUIDE

We hope that these discussion questions will enhance your
reading group's exploration of Bethany Ball's *What to Do About
the Solomons*. They are meant to stimulate discussion, offer new
viewpoints, and enrich your enjoyment of the book.

More reading group guides and additional information, including
summaries, author tours, and author sites for other fine Grove
Atlantic titles may be found on our website, groveatlantic.com.

QUESTIONS FOR DISCUSSION

One reviewer writes, "in her first novel, *What to Do About the Solomons*, Bethany Ball seems intent on asserting an inverse of Tolstoy's famous adage: All unhappy Jewish families may in fact be alike, but each happy Jewish family is happy in its own way." Share your thoughts on this adage and how it helped you to understand the Solomon family and those closest to them.

———

How does the family tree help to introduce the characters and set the stage for the rest of the novel? Discuss the relevance of the title, *What to Do About the Solomons*. The author answers the question with "The Solomons will do for themselves" (p. 243). What do you think Ball means by this? How would you have answered? Explain your thoughts.

———

How does the kibbutz function as a character in the novel? Identify and describe some of the traits of the kibbutz.

———

Why do you think people like reading about family sagas? Compare and contrast the ways in which the Solomon family differs from your own. Are there any similarities? Explain your answers.

———

Analyze the ways in which the sea functions as a symbol throughout the novel. How do Maya, Shai, and Marc's fascination with the sea help to reveal more about their characters? Provide examples found in the story.

What to do About the Solomons is a deeply complex family saga. Take a closer look at what Ball is attempting to say about the complicated relationship between family members, particularly siblings. Discuss how the characters define family. How do the Solomon children establish their identities? How are Guy and Maya used to compare and contrast with that of the Solomon siblings?

Discuss whether it is possible to read a novel with flawed and unlikeable characters and still enjoy the story. What is your favorite book(s) with unsympathetic protagonists?

Maya attempts suicide several times in the novel. Why do you think she is so intent on taking her life? Examine closely whether she may have been aware on some level of the big secret revealed later in the story?

Evaluate what Ball reveals about Marc in this passage: "The universe withholds something from Marc and it's up to him to find it again, that click, the sound of the mark found underwater as the device attaches to the ship. Marc will search forever to find it" (p. 169). What is the "click" Ball is referring to? Discuss the affect this moment has on Marc's life and the decisions he makes going forward.

Consider Dror's role in the novel as the gossip monger. How does his malicious glee at the misfortune of others function as a device to move the story along?

Yakov says, "Of all my three sons, it was Guy I loved the best. The one who was not my son. The only one I could talk to" (p. 5). Why do you suppose Yakov, and to a lesser degree Vivienne, feel such a strong connection with their son-in-law? Discuss the significance of Guy's actions in the story. Ponder the author's decision to begin and end the novel with Guy instead of one of the Solomons.

Explore the problems of inheritance and the different meanings of the word. How is the word applied to the characters in the book? Provide examples of some of the things the characters inherit throughout the novel.

The character of Tomer Skymatsky doesn't have a chapter dedicated to him, but he is a major presence in the lives of the Solomons. Discuss Tomer's connection to the sprawling cast of characters. Why do you think the author chose not to give Tomer a chapter?

The recurrent symbol of the prostitute in fiction is usually portrayed as the fallen woman who has lost her innocence. How does Ball address this archetype with the character of Carolyn? Analyze why the Solomon family doesn't like her. Which other character could also represent the role of the fallen woman? Is this reputation deserved? Explain your opinions.

Tackle the structure of the novel. The author introduces a new point of view in each chapter. How did this affect your understanding of what happens in the story? Did you find yourself empathizing with one character's perspective more than the other? Clarify your answers.

Let's take a moment to discuss what we learn about the patriarch and matriarch of the Solomon family in the "Yakov in Youth" chapter. Compare and contrast what we learn about them in this chapter with what happens later in the novel. How much have they changed? How much have they remained the same? Do you think they truly loved one another? Provide examples to support your answers.

———

Consider what the author is trying to convey here: "Marriage was an outdated concept . . . A relic. A superstition" (p. 140). Discuss what marriage means to you. What are your views of the different marriages portrayed in the novel? Are the characters in healthy, happy unions? Why or why not?

———

SUGGESTIONS FOR FURTHER READING

Saints for All Occasion: A Novel by J. Courtney Sullivan

All Grown Up by Jami Attenberg

Forest Dark by Nicole Krauss

Broken River: A Novel by J. Robert Lennon

The Leavers: A Novel by Lisa Ko

Standard Deviation: A Novel by Katherine Heiny

For the Relief of Unbearable Urges by Nathan Englander

A Visit from the Goon Squad by Jennifer Egan

Little Fires Everywhere by Celeste Ng